LIFE
WITHOUT *regret*

Ashleigh
HappyReading
xoxo
KL Grayson

K.L. GRAYSON

Live Without Regret
Copyright © 2016 by KL. Grayson

Cover Photo Photographer: Tomasz Zienkiewicz
Cover Designer: Perfect Pear Creative Covers
Editor: S.G. Thomas
KL Grayson Bio Pic Photographer: Elisabeth Wiseman Photography
Formatting by Champagne Formats

ISBN: 978-0-9907955-9-9

Dedication

To Liz.
Thank you for believing in me when I was struggling to believe in myself.

Chapter 1

Brittany

I PUSH THE DOOR OPEN AND A SMALL BELL SIGNALS my entry. At best, InkSlingers is a complete dive, not near as sleek-looking as some of the newer tattoo parlors. But this place has one thing—one person, really—that sets them above all the rest.

Connor Jackson.

Not only is he one of the most highly recommended tattoo artists in the city, but two years ago he won top prize on the reality show *Inked*. If I recall, the grand prize was two hundred thousand dollars to be used toward the establishment of his own parlor. So why in the hell he works in this dinky building off the corner of Hampton and Third, I have no idea. And to be honest, I don't really care.

"Hello?" I look around. The place is eerily quiet, not a soul in sight. Glancing down at my watch, I check the time. Sure enough, it's fifteen minutes earlier than my scheduled appointment. That's me...Miss Punctuality.

I spend the next five minutes pacing across the waiting room of the shop without seeing a single person, all the while wondering who in the hell leaves their shop unattended?

Just when I'm about ready to say screw it and walk out, the front door opens and once again the bell dings. I spin around on my heel, prepared to chew someone's ass for making me wait, and then nearly trip over my own feet when I see the behemoth of a man standing in front of me.

Without permission, my eyes rake him over from head to toe. His dirty blond hair is shaggy and clearly hasn't been trimmed for months. He could probably pull it into one of those man-bun things that seem to be all the rage, but instead it hangs loose with the stray strands tucked behind his ears.

My eyes travel south, taking in his plain black tee that stretches tight across his broad chest and even tighter around his biceps. A colorful sleeve of tattoos decorates his right arm, and as far as I can tell the left is completely bare. He's sexy, in a rugged sort of way. He's also the complete opposite of the guys I'm normally attracted to, yet I find myself enraptured.

The stranger clears his throat, and my eyes snap up to find piercing blue eyes staring back at me. When he cocks an eyebrow, I realize I've been caught checking him out. My first instinct is to avert my eyes and murmur an apology, but then I realize that's what the old Brittany would do. And I dropped her off by the curb a long time ago.

"What?" I say, shrugging unapologetically.

"Were you checking me out?" The sound of his gravelly voice does things to me that a voice should never be able to do to another human being. I squeeze my thighs together to suppress the tingling it caused.

"Well, that depends."

"On what?"

"Do you want me to check you out?" I ask.

He nods and moves past me, his shoulder grazing mine. "Bold. I like it. What can I do for you?"

Furrowing my brow, I tilt my head. I totally had him pegged for my next conquest—a.k.a. one-night stand—but I have a strange feeling he just brushed me off. I shake my head, trying to remember the question. Oh yeah. Connor. "I have a ten o'clock appointment with Connor. He's late."

The stranger looks down at his watch and then back at me. "He's not late. It's only nine fifty-five."

I roll my eyes. "Okay, fine." I walk over and plop down in a waiting room chair, then cross my legs, knee over knee. "Will you call him and see how much longer he's going to be?"

"You in a hurry?" the guy asks.

Not really. No. "Maybe."

He nods and sets his to-go coffee cup and brown paper bag on the front desk, then sits down and pulls out his phone. "He won't be long."

"Let's hope," I mumble, grabbing a *Tattoo Weekly* magazine off the table in front of me.

"Would you like a doughnut?" I glance up to see the man holding up a chocolate-covered doughnut. It looks delicious, and I'm two seconds away from accepting his offer when I remember my closet full of clothes that are becoming too tight. That one doughnut will easily take me hours at the gym to burn off.

"No, thank you."

He shrugs. "Suit yourself."

Smiling tightly, I look back at the magazine and spend the next several minutes absently thumbing through it. I skim a few articles then toss the magazine on the table and grab another, my frustration growing with each passing second.

"Are you ready?"

I glance up to find the sexy stranger standing in front of me. Putting the magazine back on the table, I look around. "Is Connor here?"

The man smiles, his full lips parting to reveal perfectly white teeth. There's a smudge of chocolate near the corner of his mouth, and I briefly wonder what he would do if I stepped forward and licked it off.

"I'm Connor," he says. His words catch me off guard and all thoughts of chocolate drift from my mind. My eyes roam his face, only this time I take a closer look.

"You're Connor?" I ask incredulously.

"Wow," he says, chuckling. "Don't look so surprised. I take it I'm not what you expected." His voice is clipped, and I instantly berate myself for the way that came out.

"No." I shake my head vehemently. "I didn't mean it in a bad way. You're an incredibly attractive man. It's just that you look different from when you were on the show. You didn't have the facial hair—or the long hair, for that matter—both of which I find unbelievably sexy." Connor's eyes widen and I realize what I said. "I can't believe I just said that. Damn it," I mumble, averting my eyes. This is what happens when I get

5

nervous, and for some strange reason, Connor makes me nervous. Sighing, I decide to give up. "I'm sorry if I offended you."

My eyes are trained on the floor as I contemplate leaving to avoid further embarrassment. I'm still undecided when a pair of Chuck T's enters my line of sight. I smile because those are my favorite shoes. "So you like the beard?" he says suggestively, causing me to look up. His blue eyes are swirling with a mixture of amusement and lust.

"I like the beard."

Connor grins as though he just found out he won a prize. Without saying a word, he steps away and I follow behind. Leading me into a small room in the back of the shop, he says, "Did you find something in the magazine that you want?"

"I actually have a picture of what I want."

"Let's see it."

I walk toward him and hold out my phone. Connor takes the phone, examines the picture then looks up.

"Where do you want it?"

"Here." Lifting my right arm, I tug my shirt up and point to the location along my rib cage, just under my breast.

"I like that," he says, handing me my phone. "But

what if we angled it just a bit like this..." Connor puts a finger at the top of my ribs and a tiny zap of electricity jolts through my body. He looks up, his eyes searching mine before he drags the tip of his index finger along my skin. His touch leaves a trail of goose bumps. My pulse quickens, and it takes everything I have not to beg him to keep touching me when he pulls away.

"What do you think?" he asks. His pupils are dilated, his breathing a bit faster, and I get the feeling he was as affected by that as I was.

"I"—my voice cracks and I flush with embarrassment—"I like it. Plus, you're the expert so I'll leave it completely up to you."

Connor swallows hard and my eyes follow the movement. "Good choice." He turns away. "All right, have a seat here," he says, gesturing toward the reclined chair, and I sit down. "Turn this way." He angles my body to the left. "Is that comfortable?"

"Yep."

"Good," he mumbles, tugging my shirt up to expose my right side again.

The soft cotton slips down and he pushes it back up, only this time his hand brushes against my bra, grazing the outside of my breast. Another jolt passes through me, only this time it's stronger. His eyes snap to mine, and I know—I *know*—that he felt *that*.

As I bite down on my bottom lip, his sinful eyes flash with heat, and I watch him take a ragged breath before turning away.

"So...is, uh, is this your first tattoo?" he stammers, bringing his eyes back to mine.

"Nope. I have another one."

"Good, so you know what to expect." I nod, and then he smiles brightly before getting his equipment ready. "Okay," he says. He rubs my skin with something cool and I presume he's prepping it. "Let's do this."

The faint whir of the machine signals this is happening, and I squeeze my eyes shut as he gently pulls my skin taut. Okay, time to go to my happy place, which just so happens to feature none other than my sexy-as-hell tattoo artist.

My mind drifts into eroticland—as I like to call it—as I picture Connor sliding his hand up my bare thigh. He hooks a finger under the side of my panties, and with his wicked eyes on me he slips a finger in—

"I like the quote," he says, pulling me from my fantasy.

"Do you know what it means?" I ask, opening my eyes and then quickly looking away. I'm a doctor, so you'd think the sight of blood wouldn't bother me. And it doesn't, as long as it isn't *my* blood.

"I've put it on a few other people. Looked it up one time. It's deep."

"Yeah"—I take a big breath, holding it in for a few beats before letting it out—"well..." My words trail off because I don't really know what else to say, and I sure as hell don't want to talk about why this particular tattoo means so much to me.

Connor goes quiet, but I can feel his eyes burning a hole through my head. When I glance up, his eyes catch mine for a brief second before he looks back down. It was just enough time to tell me that he had my number.

"So it's personal, huh?"

"What?" I scoff. "A girl can't get a tattoo just to get a tattoo?"

"Of course she can, but you're different. This is personal." He cocks his head to the side, his hair falling in front of his face. I have to fist my hands together to keep from brushing it away so that I can see his face more clearly.

"Okay, fine, you're right. It's personal."

"I'm always right," he says, a smirk tugging at the corner of his mouth. "It would be prudent of you to remember that." I tilt my head to the side just as the machine turns off and Connor looks up. He has one hand settled at the base of my waist, the other holding the tattoo gun off to the side. His eyes are smoldering, pinning me in my seat.

My tongue darts out, running a slow path along my lower lip, and I watch as his eyes follow along. *Oh yeah, this is happening.* Not one to beat around the bush, I decide to go for it. It's obvious we're attracted to each other, so there's no reason for this not to happen.

"What are you doing when you get off work?"

Connor's eyebrows push into his hairline. "Are you asking me out on a date?" he asks.

My heart clenches inside my chest and I take a deep breath, because as much as I'd like to say yes, that just isn't who I am anymore. "Nope," I state impassively. "I gave up dating."

"You don't date?" he asks incredulously.

"I fuck."

Lips parted, he nods slowly several times as though he's processing what I just said—and deciding what he's going to do about it.

"Well, that's too bad, because I gave up fucking."

His cheeks flush, probably because he realized what he just admitted to, and I can't help but laugh. "So you don't have sex?"

Connor rolls his eyes, and even though I'm not a fan of the gesture, he makes it look sexy. My guess is that he makes most things look sexy. "Of course I have sex, I just stopped fucking. I gave up the meaningless one-night stands." He shrugs. "I want more."

"Ahhh." I nod. "Well, good luck with that." Connor doesn't say another word. He puts the tattoo gun down and then holds up a mirror so I can check out my new ink. "It's perfect," I state, my eyes roaming over the beautiful script.

"I'm glad you like it." Connor puts the mirror down and slathers some Vaseline on my tattoo. He follows it up with a bandage, all the while rattling off the aftercare instructions.

"Are we done?" I ask, secretly hoping he'll tell me no. At least then I'd have a reason to stay.

"We're done." I push up from the chair. Connor nods his head toward the front desk and I follow him up there to pay. We seem to have fallen into a comfortable silence, and his presence alone is calming in a way I can't explain. I wish like hell that he would've taken me up on my offer, because I have no doubt that it would've been fucking fantastic.

Without a word, Connor swipes my card, then I sign the receipt and shove my wallet back in my purse. When I look up, Connor is watching me intently. "Thank you," I murmur.

His blue eyes are two swirling pools of liquid heat, and what I wouldn't give to dive in and beg him to change his rules for just one night. "Don't thank me," he says, shaking his head. "It was my pleasure."

We stand there for several more seconds, the air crackling around us as I search for something to say. "I'm Brittany, by the way," I say, somewhat awkwardly.

Connor grins. "I know." I furrow my brow and he points to the desk. "You made an appointment."

"Right." My phone beeps in my purse, and I decide that's my cue to leave. "Well, I better go."

"When will I see you again?" he hollers as I walk toward the door.

Spinning around, I give him my best come-hither look. "When I decide to get another tattoo."

"Or?" he asks, a grin splitting his ruggedly handsome face.

"When you decide to fuck."

His jaw nearly hits the floor.

Brittany, one. Connor, zero.

I think I'm going to like playing this game.

Chapter 2

Brittany

Three weeks later

*S*HUT UP ALREADY!

Brad—twenty-five, full-time firefighter—hasn't shut his fucking mouth since I sat down at the bar forty-five minutes ago. He needs to shut up.

You need to shut up.

Somehow, by the grace of God, I manage to keep the words from actually spilling from my mouth, which is becoming increasingly more difficult with each dirty martini. Speaking of dirty martinis...

Raising my hand, I signal the bartender for another drink. In a matter of minutes I'm back to sipping while *still* staring at Brad's mouth as he tells me about...*shit*. What the hell was he telling me about?

It's too late. The Mississippi native with a sexy Southern drawl has officially bored me to death. My shoulders deflate, and I take another drink. This is pointless. As much as I'd like to rip off Brad's clothes to see if his body is as chiseled as it looks, I just can't get past the fact that he's unable to hold my interest in a simple conversation.

It's probably my fault. I'm the one who asked him to tell me about himself, and now I have to figure out how in the hell to get him to stop.

"Brittany." Brad snaps his fingers and I look up, catching his gaze. He smiles a thousand-watt smile, and for a fraction of a second I reconsider my decision to ditch him.

"I'm sorry," I say sheepishly. "I, uhh...I must've zoned out. What was the question?"

"He asked if he could take you out on a date." My head whips to the right at the familiar voice. Looks like the night just got a whole lot more interesting.

Connor's blue eyes lock on mine. "I take it you haven't told him yet."

I have no idea what he's up to, but I decide to take the bait. "I'm not sure I know what you're talking about." Raising my eyebrows, I wrap my lips around the rim of my glass and take a sip. Connor cocks a brow, his gorgeous eyes dancing with mischief.

"She doesn't date." He directs his words at Brad. "She fucks."

My eyes leave Connor's long enough to see Brad perk up in his seat.

"You don't date?" Brad asks.

"I don't," I tell him.

"She fucks," Connor clarifies.

Brad nods, his brown eyes now thick with lust. "She fucks," he says slowly as though he's trying to understand what Connor just said.

Connor grins. "But not you."

"Why not me?"

Shifting in my seat, I narrow my gaze on Connor. "Yeah, why not him?"

"Do you want to fuck him?" he fires back, tossing a thumb toward Brad.

"Now wait a minute," Brad says as he slides off his chair. In one stealthy and incredibly sexy move, Connor pushes his way between Brad and me, effectively blocking out our third wheel. His hands land on either side of my chair and he bends down until we're eye to eye. As his breath fans my face, I wonder if he tastes as good as he smells.

"Have a drink with me?" he asks.

Holding up my martini glass, I give a little wave. "I am having a drink."

Connor pushes against my legs and I automatically part them, allowing him to step in between. Heaven help me, he feels good settled between my thighs. I just wish we could resume this position later sans clothes. "Have a drink with me over there," he says, nodding toward a booth.

"Like a date?"

He shakes his head, a grin pulling at the corner of his mouth. "Well, since you don't date, I know better than to ask you out on one. It's just a drink. Two, if I'm lucky."

"Excuse me." Brad steps around Connor, who throws up a hand.

"We're not done," Connor says dismissively.

Brad's eyes widen and flick to mine. I need to put the poor boy out of his misery. As much as I'd love to spend a few nights with him warming my bed, it's probably a lost cause. He's too young, and I'm not ready to be classified as a cougar. Not yet anyway.

Setting my drink on the bar, I push up from my seat. Connor's face falls when he's forced to move back. I smooth my hands down the front of my blouse and step up to Brad. This is the part I hate.

Rejection. Been there. Done that. I've got a broken heart to prove it.

And that's exactly why I need to do this now. "Thank you for the drink," I say, knowing that honesty is always the best policy. Out of the corner of my eye, I see Connor grin. "I think you're a great guy, but this"—I wave a hand between the two of us—"isn't going to happen."

I don't give Brad a chance to reply, because giving him that chance also gives him hope ... and there is no hope. Spinning around, I come face-to-face with Connor. "I'm ready for that drink," I say. His grin grows into a breathtaking smile, causing my heart to stutter inside my chest. "Or two."

Connor grabs my hand, and I snag my drink from the bar. He leads us toward a booth tucked in a corner where we slide in opposite each other. I glance toward the bar, thankful when I see a busty blonde sidle up next to Brad. I knew it wouldn't take him long.

"Hi." Connor's smooth voice rolls over me, wrapping me up like a warm blanket.

Turning my attention to Connor, I smile. "Hi."

"I'm starting to think you're stalking me." He smirks before quickly adding, "Which, for the record, I'm totally cool with."

"Funny, because I was just thinking the exact

same thing."

"That I'm stalking you or that you'd be totally cool with me stalking you?" Connor's playful words, coupled with my alcohol-infused state, cause me to let down my guard.

"Both." I lean forward, placing my elbows on the table, and Connor mimics my position. His woodsy scent floats through the air and I take a deep breath, trying to memorize the smell. "Have you changed your mind?" I ask.

"Funny, I was just thinking the exact same thing," he says, tossing my words back at me.

Lifting my glass, I take a sip. It's the only way to keep myself from smiling like a fucking idiot, which is exactly what I want to do. "So"—I set my glass down—"do you come here often?"

Connor blinks several times, the look on his face telling me he wasn't expecting me to say that. Honestly, it isn't what I wanted to say. What I wanted to say was '*hell yes, I've changed my mind,*' but I knew better. My heart remembers the sharp pain that lanced through it, effectively slicing it into thousands of tiny pieces. It remembers the sound of my cries as I begged Tyson to stay, to love me, to choose me. Worse yet, it knows I don't have a heart left to give away.

"As a matter of fact, I do come here often. How

about you?" he asks, absently peeling at the label on his beer bottle. "I don't think I've seen you here before."

"You haven't," I confirm, shaking my head. "I moved back a few months ago."

"So you grew up here in St. Louis?"

"I grew up across the river on the Illinois side, but, yes, this is home." I'm reluctant to give him much more than that because it'll lead to talking about what brought me home, and that's something I'm not ready to discuss. He doesn't need to know my fiancé walked out on me, and he sure as hell doesn't need to know it took me two years to pick myself up from that devastating blow. So instead, I decide to redirect the conversation. "Are you from—?"

"There you are," Casey breathes. Sliding into the booth next to me, she pushes a chunk of hair out of her face. "I was looking everywhere for you." She glances up and freezes when she sees Connor sitting across from us. Her eyes widen, a grin playing at the corner of her mouth. "You aren't Brad, the firefighter."

Connor laughs and shakes his head. "Connor, the tattoo artist," he says, reaching his hand across the table. She slips her hand in his and this weird twisting sensation takes place inside my chest. I thought I had gotten rid of that green-eyed monster. Guess I was wrong.

I don't like them touching.

Why the fuck don't I like them touching?

My first instinct is to shove Casey out of the booth or accidentally spill my drink in her lap, but I quickly push the thoughts away because those are things a jealous girlfriend would do.

And I am *not* a jealous girlfriend. Plus, Casey is my sister…whom I love…dearly.

Hell, I'm not even *a* girlfriend.

But I do need to do something because she's smiling and—*shit*—now he's smiling. And they're still touching.

Why in the world are they still touching?

"Where's Mike?" My words are rushed, my voice clipped, but it does the job. Casey releases Connor's hand and I sigh in relief. I should feel better, but I don't. In fact, now I'm really pissed off at myself for getting jealous.

"Mike who?" Casey says, interrupting my thoughts.

"The guy you were just molesting out on the dance floor. Remember him?"

Casey tilts her head to the side, narrowing her eyes. For a split second, I'm certain she sees right through me. And she might. Not only is she my baby sister, but she's also my best friend and knows me better than anyone.

"Oh, right. Mike. He was no one." She shakes her head and quickly waves me off, returning her attention to Connor. "So, Connor, how do you know my sister?"

I peek up at Connor. *Please say you're the man who's going to be spending the night with me,* I silently beg. "You two are sisters?" he asks, motioning toward us.

I nod. "We are."

"I," Casey says, pointing toward herself, "am the younger, sweeter, smarter sister. *Oomph.*" She grunts when I elbow her in the side and then she giggles. "You still haven't answered my question, Connor."

Connor takes a swig of his beer. "I'm her tattoo artist."

"*What?*" Connor winces at Casey's loud screech. I'm used to the sound, having lived with the crazy broad my whole life. "You have a tattoo?"

"Actually, I have two," I say proudly, holding up two fingers.

"When did this happen?" she asks, looking from me to Connor and back to me. "And why am I just finding out about it now?"

Connor holds up his hands and slowly shakes his head. "Hey, I'm only responsible for the second one.

I wasn't the lucky son-of-a-bitch who got to pop that cherry."

Warmth radiates up my neck, infusing my cheeks, and Connor's heated gaze slides to mine. To avoid his penetrating eyes, I look down. My body tingles—literally fucking tingles—under the weight of his stare.

"I like you," Casey states. "And you just made my sister blush, which I've never seen. I feel like you should get some sort of prize for that."

Lips pursed, I look up. "I'm not blushing."

"Right," Casey says, drawing out the word while slowly nodding. A knowing smile slides across her face. "It's just hot in here."

"It *is* hot in here," I argue.

Connor clears his throat. "I'm not hot."

Casey's head whips around and she points a finger at Connor. "Uh, yes. Yes, you are." Connor grins at the compliment.

My head drops and I bury my face in my hands. I love my sister, but her inability to filter what comes out of her mouth can be a bit annoying. "Go get me a drink," I mumble, nudging her out of the booth. She sighs but eventually gives in.

"Fine, but only because *I* need a drink." I look up as Casey turns to Connor. "Do you want another beer?" she asks.

"That'd be great." Connor holds up his beer bottle to show her what he's drinking. "Just put it all on my tab."

"Connor, the tattoo artist, you are too kind." She flashes him a flirty smile and struts—yes, struts—toward the bar.

Connor nods toward Casey. "I like your sister."

"You can have her."

"I heard that," Casey yells. "And you would miss the hell out of me," she tosses over her shoulder before reaching the bar.

I shake my head and mouth 'no.' Connor's answering smile is enough to make my insides go all soft and gooey, something I haven't experienced in a long time. What I wouldn't give to feel that every single day. What I wouldn't give to know I was the one who put that smile on Connor's face—the kind of smile that, if allowed, could mend broken hearts. The kind of smile that could make a girl hope for things she shouldn't be hoping for, like white picket fences, blond-haired babies, and the promise of forever. Except…

Forever doesn't exist.

Forever can be taken away.

Minds can change, and in the blink of an eye, everything you thought you had simply disappears.

Shit.

Why the hell am I thinking about forever? Surely his smile isn't that potent.

"You can't smile at me like that," I whisper. Then I squeeze my eyes shut when I realize I actually said those words out loud. I've been so good about closing myself off, putting on my armor and shielding myself from feeling...well, anything.

But Connor is different. He's a game changer. When I'm around him, I want to rip down all of my walls and try.

Try what? I'm not sure. Anything, maybe. Anything other than what I've been doing. And it's not that I want to try with just anyone, I want to try with *him*.

"You don't like it when I smile?" he asks, his husky voice invading my thoughts.

Opening my eyes, I glance up. His eyes are smoldering, begging me to give him what he wants. Who am I to disappoint? My head is screaming...

Mayday!

Abort!

Look away!

But my heart isn't listening. "I love it when you smile."

Connor's eyes widen and he goes completely still.

Oh, God. Why in the hell did I just say that?

He's probably confused with all of these mixed

signals I keep throwing out. Hell, so am I.

Connor hasn't said a word and he's still watching me. I've seen that look before. I saw it on Tyson—several times, in fact—years before he ripped my heart out.

Fix this, Brit.

My eyes drift to the dance floor. I can't help but feel like I'd be much safer out there in the midst of all those gyrating bodies than I am here sitting in this booth, looking into the eyes of this man who sees way too much. This man who makes me say stupid, *stupid* things.

Looking at him isn't an option, because if I look at him, I'll cave. So I do the only thing I can do—the only thing that will preserve what willpower I have left.

I ease out of the booth. "I'm going to go dance."

Chapter 3

Connor

WHAT JUST HAPPENED?

"Where the hell is she going?" Scooting into the seat Brittany just vacated, Casey hands me a beer, but her eyes are locked on her sister's retreating form.

"I'm an asshole." A *fucking* asshole.

Brittany's blatant honesty caught me off guard and I froze. She had made it clear that she wasn't into dating, only meaningless sex. Therefore, I expected her to brush off my question, or at the very least come up with some sort of sarcastic answer. But the vulnerability on her face when she said she loved my smile was unmistakable, and it left me at a loss for words.

I had been seconds away from telling her that I'd gladly have meaningless sex with her if the offer still stood. The need to touch her was growing by the second, and although I would've hated myself in the morning, I was willing to take whatever she would give me.

But then I saw it. The truth behind whatever façade she was putting up was short-lived, but it was all I needed. I knew right then and there that if I played my cards right, I could break down her walls ... and I desperately want to break down her walls.

"Most men are," she mumbles. We both watch as Brittany finds an empty spot on the dance floor and starts moving her body in perfect rhythm with the music. "But," she says, turning toward me, "I have a feeling that you, sir, are a redeemable asshole."

Choosing not to comment, I take a drink of my beer. I know I'm not really an asshole, and I can tell by the tone of Casey's voice she doesn't think that either.

"She likes to think she's made for meaningless sex," Casey says, confirming what I had begun to suspect. "But she isn't. It's not who she is. She's been hurt, and this is her way of protecting herself."

Casey takes a sip of her purple concoction. When I open my mouth to respond, she holds up a hand, signaling me to wait. Lowering her glass to the table, she twirls it between her fingers. "There are two things you should know about my sister. First," she says, holding up a finger, "she can't—and I repeat *cannot*— say no to the Cardinals." I furrow my brows, completely confused as to what the Cardinals have to do with anything. Before I can ask, Casey quickly continues. "And second, when it comes right down to it, she will *always* follow her heart. Now," she says, sliding from the booth, drink in hand. "That's all you need to know to land my sister. What you do with it is completely up to you. But"—she points a finger at me—"if you break her heart, I will hunt you down and do godawful things to your manhood." Without a second glance, she spins on her heel and walks away.

For the second time in a matter of minutes, a woman has rendered me speechless. But this time I don't let the girl get away. "Why are you helping me?" I ask.

Casey stops mid-step and looks over her shoulder. "Because I love my sister more than anyone else in this world, and I saw a spark in her eyes tonight that I haven't seen in over two years. I want to see that spark every day, Connor." I have absolutely no idea what to say to that, so I nod. "Now"—Casey gestures toward the dance floor—"you better go get your girl before some other asshole snags her." With a quick wink, she walks away.

Tipping my head back, I drain what's left of my beer then scoot out from behind the table. I may be an asshole, but I'm a smart asshole, and she doesn't have to tell me twice.

I stand up and walk toward the edge of the dance floor. It isn't big, but you'd never know by the number of bodies currently inhabiting the small space. It doesn't take long to locate Brittany, and not because my eyes are drawn to her like a magnet—which they are—but because she's the one with men circling her, waiting to stake their claim.

She's completely oblivious to the attention she's getting, and for some reason I find that insanely attractive. Brittany has a kick-ass body that most women would pay ridiculous amounts of money for, and she isn't even using it to get what she could clearly have—what she stated she wants.

Her head is tilted back, eyes closed, and when the beat of the song shifts, she tosses a hand up in the air. Slowly, she lowers her hand, threading her fingers into her straight blonde hair as her hips roll from side to side.

I've watched women dance before. Hell, I've even had a few lap dances, but nothing compares to watching *this* woman dance. It's the sexiest thing I've ever seen and my cock swells against the confines of my zipper. Without bothering to hide it, I adjust myself and take a step toward Brittany. The guy next to me must be thinking the exact same thing because he too takes a step in her direction.

Ain't fuckin' happening.

I hold my arm out and it bumps him in the chest. "She's taken, bro," I say. His reply is nothing but muffled noise because I don't stick around to listen. In three long strides, I'm standing behind Brittany.

Heat from her body is rolling off in waves. She smells like a mixture of sweat and tropical flowers with a hint of summer, and it's hands down the most intoxicating fragrance I've ever encountered. Unable to keep my distance, I step toward her until the front of my body molds against her back. She doesn't look to see who it is, but she doesn't move away either. I'm not sure if that makes me happy or insanely jealous.

Does she know it's me? Does she feel the same strange sensation in her chest when we're within arm's reach of each other? Or would she dance with just anyone pressed against her backside?

Our bodies move together for several beats, her hips rocking from side to side. Gripping her waist with my right hand, I pull her body flush with mine. Her ass pushes against my groin and she gasps.

Lowering my mouth to her ear, I whisper, "That's what you do to me." Her body shivers at the sound of my voice, and when her head drops to my chest, I push my hips forward.

Looking down, I see Brittany's eyes flutter open and then her eyes lock on mine. Her chest rises and falls with each sharp intake of breath, and that's when I know she's just as affected as I am. The music keeps playing, but our bodies are no longer moving. Everything around us fades away. All of the other bodies—gone. It's just this insanely sexy woman and me. I wait patiently for her to make her move and then, as though the DJ himself knew exactly what we needed, the music shifts and everything changes.

"Ride" by Chase Rice pumps through the speakers. Brittany spins in my arms until her ample chest is pressed snugly against mine. She regards me quietly for several seconds and then her eyes drop to my mouth.

Hell yeah.

I slowly run my tongue along my bottom lip, and I'll be damned if she didn't just whimper.

"You're teasing me, Mr. Jackson." Her words come out all breathy as she drags her gaze to mine.

"Trust me"—I slide my arm around her waist and

she comes willingly when I pull her in close—"there are a lot of things going on right now, but teasing isn't one of them."

Brittany closes her eyes. She takes a shuddery breath and blows it out, drawing my attention to her pouty lips. Without thinking twice, I dip my head until my lips brush hers.

Chapter 4

Brittany

*O*H MY...

We're kissing.

Connor Jackson's lips are on mine. It's not much of a kiss—*yet*—and it's already the best kiss I've ever had. If that isn't a scary fucking thought, then I don't know what is.

My hands slide up his shirt and I splay my fingers across his broad chest. But instead of pushing him away—which I had every intention of doing—I curl my fingers into the soft flannel and hold on for dear life.

The kiss is soft, sweet, and unlike anything I expected from this tatted-up man. A rush of emotions pulse through my veins, and the need to be closer to Connor, to feel his body against mine, is all-consuming. Winding my hands around his neck, I tangle my fingers in his hair. A low groan rumbles from somewhere deep in his chest.

That sound…*holy shit that sound*. I want to hear it again.

My tongue swipes along the seam of his lips and he opens up. Tilting my head to the side, I give him full control and he doesn't hesitate to take the reins. The fact that we're making out on a dance floor in the middle of a crowded bar should bother me. It doesn't. I don't care who sees us. In fact, if his tongue keeps doing that swirly thing it's doing, I'll likely let him have his way with me right here and now.

Connor pulls back far too soon. I groan in frustration and the bastard has the nerve to chuckle. Fisting my hand in his hair, I try to yank his mouth back to mine but he resists. Instead, his hot mouth finds its way to my neck. Trailing his lips along my jaw, he finds my ear. "I changed my mind," he whispers.

His words slam into me. There's no need for Connor to explain or elaborate. I know what he's referring to, and it's exactly what I wanted.

Right?

So why does it feel so wrong? Why do I have this strong urge to get to know him, and why in the world do I have this strange feeling that one night with him won't be enough?

I shouldn't, but I want to know what makes him tick. I want to know what makes him smile, what makes him angry. I want to know what his favorite color is and what Christmas traditions he treasures most. I want to know every little thing that will cause him to make that sexy rumble I love so much.

Hope sparks deep in my chest, and it's that hope that should have me running for the hills. It serves as a reminder of why I made my rule to begin with, which in turn leads me to grabbing Connor's hand. He glances at our joined hands and then back at me.

"My place or yours?" I ask. Without waiting for an answer, I all but drag him toward the door. I need to get this over with in the slowest possible way. Meaning, I need to cherish every second with Connor because I can't allow myself to have him after tonight. I'm in too deep…and I don't even know his middle name. That alone spells disaster. But I'm weak and can't walk away. This thirst I have for him has been growing since we met in his shop three weeks ago, and tonight I'm going to quench it.

As we approach the door, I glance over my shoulder, expecting to see hesitation on Connor's face. There is none. Squaring his shoulders, he smiles confidently, and when I cock a brow, urging him to answer, he says just one word: "Mine."

Hell yes, I'm yours…for tonight.

I don't bother to tell him I only live a couple of miles away, because his place is probably a better choice. At least this way I can make a clean break when it's over.

Connor leads me to his car, and in a matter of seconds we're speeding away. Pulling my phone out of my pocket, I check the compartment on the back of my case, ensuring my ID and credit card are still firmly in place. Then I shoot Casey a quick text.

Me: Left with Connor. We're going back to his place. Leave your phone on; you'll have to come get me later.

Her reply is almost immediate.

Casey: Good for you. It's about time your vagina gets a workout.

Me: My vagina gets regular workouts, thank you very much.

Casey: BOB doesn't count.

I shake my head, smiling. How does she know I have a battery-operated boyfriend? I choose not to reply to that comment though, because you get Casey started on something and she won't stop.

Casey: Where does Connor, the tattoo artist, live?

Good question. I look up at the same time Connor makes a left-hand turn. Squinting, I focus on the street sign to see where exactly we are.

Davenport Way.

Hold up.

Davenport Way?

"You live out here?" I ask as we pass a familiar line of duplexes.

"I do," he says, turning onto Baylor Hills Drive.

"Nice neighborhood." Connor drives by yet another familiar street and I shoot off one more text to Casey.

Me: Not sure I'll need you to pick me up. I'll explain in the morning. Be good tonight. Love you.

"Thanks," he says. I tuck my phone in my pocket and look up as he pulls into a driveway.

No fucking way.

Stepping out of the car, I shut the door and stare at Connor's duplex. I don't hear him walk toward me, but I know he's there. I can feel him. The hair on my neck stands up any time he gets close, and my heart starts bouncing around inside my chest as though it's trying to get his attention.

I take a deep breath. "Are you sure this is what you want?" I ask, giving him an out and secretly hoping he'll take it. As much as I want to spend one night— *this* night—with Connor, I know that one of us is going to end up getting hurt, and it won't be me. I won't let it be me.

Connor's warm hand wraps around mine. My knees go weak at the soft, unexpected touch. "I won't lie. I want nothing more than for you to throw your rules out the window." I try to remove my hand from his, but Connor only tightens his grip. "But," he says, laughing at my weak attempt to get away, "I understand you have your rules for a reason. I wish I knew what that reason was so I could find a way to push past it, but I realize that isn't what you want and I respect that."

The wind picks up, blowing a strand of hair in front of my face. Connor drops my hand and brushes the hair from my eyes. "Ready?" His voice is strained, and a part of me wonders if it's because he wants this just as badly as I do or if it's because he knows he's making a mistake.

I pause, giving myself the opportunity to walk away, but apparently my feet have a different agenda. Because when Connor grabs my hand and leads me toward his door, I follow.

With one hand still connected to mine, Connor unlocks his door and pushes it open. We step inside, and when he walks to the left to flick on the lights, I step further into the open space and toss my phone on the entryway table.

His home is gorgeous, and not at all like the bachelor pad I expected. The walls are a deep blue accented with dark wood trim, and the room is filled with oversized, chocolate-colored furniture. It fits Connor perfectly, but it's almost *too* perfect.

I look closer to find that the mantel is adorned with framed pictures and knickknacks. A vase filled with fresh flowers sits on a hutch tucked in the corner. Intricately decorated throw pillows adorn the couch and a fluffy blue afghan is draped over the arm of the recliner. All of the details indicate a woman's touch, but what woman? A sister, a mother, an old girlfriend…a best friend, maybe?

That last thought is like a bucket of ice water being dumped on my head, and I'm reminded why it doesn't matter who decorated this place. This is the last time I'll be here.

Squaring my shoulders, I turn to find Connor standing off to the side, his eyes igniting a fire as they roam over my body. I stalk toward him until his back is pressed against the wall. His gaze drops to my mouth, but I don't give him a chance to think, let alone react. I seal my lips over his and our tongues collide, instantly dueling for power. Sliding, pushing, and sucking, neither of us is willing to give up control.

Connor tastes like pure fucking heaven.

Connor shouldn't taste like pure fucking heaven.

Tearing my lips away from his, I slide them across his jaw. Dragging my mouth to his ear, I nip at it playfully before sucking the soft flesh into my mouth. "Bedroom. Now," I whisper.

Strong arms wrap around my waist and lift me off the ground. As he takes off down the hall, I lock my ankles behind his back then claim his mouth in a heated kiss. He growls in response, and before I know it I'm wedged between the wall and a rock hard body with Connor's erection cradled between my thighs. Tilting my hips, I grind against him.

He pulls his lips from mine. "You're killing me," he says, trailing his mouth down the side of my neck. The sound of his gravelly voice shoots straight to my clit, and I push against him harder, trying to ease the ache.

"Easy," he murmurs. "We've got all night."

The scruff on his face scrapes against the sensitive skin of my neck when he talks, and it's like nothing I've ever felt before. *More. I want more.*

I open my mouth to tell him I can't wait—that I want him right here, right now. But then he pulls the front of my shirt down, exposing my white lace bra, and all thoughts flee from my brain.

"That's sexy as hell, but I want what's underneath," he says, tugging the bra down as well. My breasts pop out and he places open-mouthed kisses around one of my nipples, then blows lightly. My nipple tightens and Connor grins before bringing his lips back to my breast and devouring it. The sight proves to be too much and I drop my head back against the wall, thrusting my chest into his face. He laves one breast and then moves on to the next, all the while torturing me with slow circular motions and tiny nips.

Against my belly his erection grows, along with my desire to touch him. Dipping my hand between our bodies, I flick the button of his jeans open and lower the zipper. Connor releases my nipple with a wet pop, and keeping me anchored against the wall, he pulls his hips back enough for me to shove his pants down. Rock solid and throbbing, his erection bobs heavily between us and I wrap my fingers around his length and stroke several times. Pushing his body flush against mine, Connor drops his face to the crook of my neck. He pumps his hips, thrusting himself into my hand. We're both panting as our bodies fight to get closer, desperate for some sort of release.

"Fuck," he growls, sinking his teeth into the side of my neck.

I had no idea that giving a guy a hand job could be so erotic. Then again, I guess it isn't what I'm doing...it's who I'm doing it to. Connor's warm breath against my neck and the grunts that keep rumbling from his chest tell me he's close, but I don't want him to get off in my hand.

I release my grip on his cock. Looking up, he furrows his brows, then reluctantly lets go of my legs and I lower them to the ground. Warm hands wrap around my upper arms, steadying me until I find my balance. When I've regained some control, I nudge Connor across the hall until his back meets the opposite wall. My fingers trail up his shirt and I slowly work my way back down, undoing each button as I go. The soft flannel falls open and I can't help it—I have to get a better look at this crazy beautiful man.

Smoothing my hands over the hard plane of his

abdomen, I sweep them up his chest, pushing his shirt off in the process. My eyes are drawn to an intricate tattoo etched across the left side of his ribs. Bending at the knees, I take a closer look. It's a detailed tribal cross with a set of angel wings coming out from behind it. My fingers skate across his skin, following the black lines. Connor shivers, goose bumps breaking out across his body under the touch of my hand. His eyes follow my every movement as he allows me to explore his body.

Pressing my lips against his skin, I place a kiss to the center of the cross and then slowly drag my mouth across his chest, stopping to tease each of his nipples before kissing a path down his stomach. My tongue flicks out, outlining the chiseled lines of his abs before tracing along that sexy V that leads straight to the good. Then I slowly drop to my knees.

"Brittany." His voice sounds tortured when my name falls from his lips. Connor sinks his fingers into my hair, and the closer my mouth gets to his cock, the tighter his grip gets. The muscles of his stomach tighten beneath my touch, and I revel in the knowledge that I'm affecting him this way.

The weight of Connor's stare is heavy against my head, and I want nothing more than to look up. But I can't—at least not yet. Instead, I finally give in to what we both want. Wrapping my fingers around his hard length, I pump him several times, giving a slight twist of my wrist as I do.

A jumbled mess of words emanates from Connor, but I can't make out what he's saying. My heart is thumping loudly in my ears and pure, hot desire is pulsing through my veins.

Running my thumb along the head of his cock, I rub at the bead of cum that has formed on the tip before I flick out my tongue to taste it.

"Shit," Connor grinds out. He's losing control—I can hear it in his voice. And if that isn't the best damn feeling, then I don't know what is.

Slipping the head of his cock inside my mouth, I push my tongue against the underside of his shaft and take him deep into my mouth.

"Ah, fuck," he groans. The words are followed by a loud thud, and I finally allow myself to look up.

Connor's head is against the wall and he looks sexy as hell. His eyes are squeezed tightly shut, and I watch for several seconds as his chest heaves with each breath he takes. Sucking hard, I work him faster and deeper. He grows impossibly large inside my mouth, and his abs flex with each pump of my hand. The sight of him losing control is almost too much, causing a strangled moan to rip from my throat.

His eyelids flutter open and Connor looks down under a hooded gaze. "Deeper," he demands. "Take more of me."

What woman in her right mind could ever say no to that? Sure as hell not this woman.

Curling my lips around my teeth, I push deeper. His cock bottoms out at the back of my throat and Connor grunts. "Fuck yeah. Just like that." His words send a surge of heat straight to my pussy and I close my thighs as best I can.

A few strands of my hair fall forward, blocking my view of his gorgeous face, and he reaches out to sweep the strands to the side. With one hand buried in my hair and the other cupping my cheek, he watches me take him over and over into my mouth.

"Sexiest thing I've ever seen," he rasps. "Watching your sweet little mouth take my cock like that..." His eyes close as his words trail off and I silently beg him to continue. I've never been one for dirty talk, but from him I *love* it.

The silence is filled with soft moans, and then Connor's entire body jerks and his eyes pop open. Dropping his hand from my cheek, he links his fingers at the back of my head, urging me to pick up the pace as his hips thrust forward.

"I'm not gonna last," he says, gritting his teeth.

I can't remember the last time I actually watched a man lose himself to the pleasure of a woman. Honestly, it's not something I ever gave much thought to, but I want to watch *this* man. I want to watch as Connor surrenders himself to my mouth—*to me*.

His body goes rigid beneath the weight of my hands and his grip on my head loosens, presumably giving me the opportunity to pull back.

No way in hell.

My cheeks hollow, my tongue pushing his cock against the roof of my mouth as I suck long and hard. With a string of incoherent words, Connor finally lets go and I suck him dry, savoring every last drop he has to offer.

Chapter 5

Brittany

CONNOR PULLS ME UP OFF THE FLOOR. ONE HAND pressed against the small of my back, the other cradling my head, he hauls me in close. Then he smiles, slow and sexy. "What am I going to do with you?" he asks, sealing his lips over mine.

Unlike the last kiss, this one isn't hurried. It's slow, methodical, and utterly intoxicating. Skimming my hands up his arms, I tangle them in his hair. I've never been with a man whose hair is long, but I'm finding it incredibly inviting. Plus, it'll give me something to hold onto when he has his head buried between my thighs.

Hell, Connor's hair isn't the only thing that sets him apart. My previous conquests have been perfectly groomed, suit or scrub-wearing types that wouldn't dream of having a tattoo, much less a body covered in them. Maybe that's where I was going wrong with men. Maybe all along I just needed someone more like Connor.

What the hell am I talking about?

I don't need a man. I have a hard enough time keeping myself in check, let alone having to worry about a man.

This is all Connor's fault. If it weren't for his seductive mouth, I wouldn't be having these crazy thoughts. Damn his lips for being so hypnotizing.

Giving his hair a tug, I pull Connor's head back. His eyelids bob heavily several times. "Bedroom," I say, my lips brushing his. "I need—" A loud noise rings throughout the house, interrupting me, and I cock my head to the side. "Is that a house phone? Do you have a landline?" I curl my lips into my mouth, trying to suppress a smile at the look of disbelief on Connor's face.

"Yes," he says chuckling as he pulls his pants up. He leaves them unbuttoned, which I assume is an invitation to get back into them later. "And don't you laugh at me. It's connected to my shop phone so I can take calls and appointments when I'm home." I stare blankly at him. "People still have house phones," he states firmly.

I shake my head. "Most people don't have house phones."

Connor takes a step forward, nudging me back. "Are you making fun of me?" he asks with a sly look on his face.

The phone rings one last time before the answering machine picks up. Connor's voice filters through the air, but the caller hangs up. And that's when I start giggling. I can't help it. Slapping a hand over my mouth, I fail at trying to hold in my amusement, and the look on Connor's face does nothing but make me laugh harder.

"I can't believe you're making fun of me."

Maybe it's the low level of alcohol still sifting through my body, or perhaps it's all of the pent-up emotion I've been holding in lately. Or maybe it's Connor and the way his eyes are softening as he watches me, but I tip my head back and let out the most unladylike snort known to mankind.

"Did you just snort?" Connor asks, making me snort again.

"I did." I gasp, nodding like a damn bobblehead. "I totally snorted." I take a few deep breaths to calm myself down. Wiping the tears of laughter from my face,

I glance at Connor. Something in his expression has changed. He's no longer looking at me like he wants to ravage me, and his face is void of any amusement. Instead, his eyes are warm and inviting.

The phone starts ringing again, and I point toward the other room. "Do you need to answer that?"

Connor shakes his head. "I don't care who it is," he says, taking another step toward me.

"All I care about right now is this beautiful woman standing in front of me."

Oh.

Oh my.

That was good.

Connor's eyes rake down my body and then back up again. He looks like a man who is in desperate need of food, and I'm his next meal. I don't remember the last time a man looked at me like this, but I want *him* to look at me like this all the time.

But he can't if you don't give him a chance.

And just like that, my resolve crumbles. Because as much as I hate to break my own rules, I hate the thought of never seeing Connor again even more. The thought of letting my own fears keep me from what could potentially be something great makes my stomach roll. Plus, if any man is worth taking that chance on, it has to be this man. The one I can't stop thinking about, and the one who makes me wish for things I'd long ago given up on.

And let's not forget the butterflies.

A big, huge swarm of them that take flight every single time he looks at me.

I haven't felt that ... *ever*.

Two years is long enough, so I decide to go with my gut—or maybe it's my heart. Right now I think they're working together, plotting against me. *Damn conspirators.*

Swallowing hard past the lump in my throat, I say the words before I chicken out. "I change my mind," I whisper.

Connor's eyes widen, and in a flash I'm scooped up in his arms. But instead of walking down the hall toward where I imagine the bedroom would be, he walks into the living room. Sitting down on the couch, Connor settles me on his lap. I straddle his hips and bring my hands to the front of his shirt.

"This isn't the bedroom," I state, leaning forward to place a kiss on his plump lips.

Connor allows me to have my way with his mouth, and when I finally pull back to take a breath, he chuckles. "If I would've known it'd only take a blow job to get you to change your mind, then I would've obliged at the tattoo shop."

I slap playfully at his arm. "The blow job had nothing to do with it." The answering machine kicks on for the second time and I smile before continuing. "It was all you and that damn smile," I say, kissing him again because, well…I can.

"Connor, the tattoo artist…" Gasping, I slap a hand over my mouth as my sister's voice fills the room. "Brittany isn't answering her phone, or her texts, and I am *not* happy about it. Did you know your buddy Todd is an asshole? Because he is. He wouldn't give me your damn number. Do you know what I had to do to get him to give me your number?" she asks.

"Who's Todd?" I whisper, lowering my hand.

"He owns the bar we were at earlier," Connor answers as Casey continues with her tirade.

"I had to *flash* him," Casey scoffs. "Can you believe that? The little shit wouldn't give me your damn number until I agreed to flash him. Unbelievable. Anyway," she says with a yawn, as if flashing Todd was no big deal. "Brit, if you're there, I really need you to come home. I locked myself out of the house—" The answering machine beeps, cutting Casey off mid-sentence. Scooting off Connor's lap, I grab my phone from the entryway table and shoot her a quick text.

Me: Be there in one minute.

"I'm so sorry," I say, straightening my clothes.

"But I've gotta go."

Connor stands up, buttons his pants, and smooths out his rumpled shirt. "I'll take you home," he says, grabbing his keys from the hook next to the door.

As much as I hate to leave, this next part should be fun. "You don't have to take me home, I can walk. It's not far."

"Hell no," he says, shaking his head. "It's after midnight. No way am I letting you walk home."

"It's really not necess—"

Connor's big blue eyes fill with uncertainty. "Did you change your mind?" he asks, cutting me off.

"No," I breathe, shaking my head. "Did you change your mind?" I'm hoping he'll say no, because I wouldn't bend my rules for just anyone and I really, *really* like him.

Connor takes a step toward me, wraps me in his arms, and pulls me in close until we're nose to nose. "Not even close. Tonight was…"

"Tonight was what?" I ask.

Connor kisses me softly once…twice…and then a third time before pulling back. He licks his lips and runs the back of his fingers along my cheek. "You taste amazing."

"Tonight was what?" I ask again. I want to know what he's thinking, and I need to hear the words.

"It was fucking incredible." Warm hands cup my cheeks. "I want to do it again. *A lot.*"

I bust up laughing. "You want a lot more blow jobs?"

"No...well, yes." He starts laughing, too. "I want more of you. I want to get to know you. Let me take you out on a real date."

"An official first date, huh? Where would you take me?"

"Is that a yes?"

"Yes," I answer. Just knowing I'm going to get to spend more time with Connor causes my chest to fill with warmth.

"I was thinking maybe—"

My phone beeps with an incoming text, cutting Connor off. "Shit," I hiss. "I bet that's Casey."

Connor releases his hold and I shiver at the loss of his touch.

Casey: It's been three minutes. Where the hell are you? I have to pee.

"I've gotta go." Bolting for the front door, I yank it open. Connor yells my name as I slip out the door, down his steps, and jog across the tiny patch of grass before stopping in front of my side of the duplex. Casey is sitting cross-legged on our porch, her back propped against the door.

"Where the hell did you come fr—?" She stops abruptly, her eyes cutting over my shoulder. Connor must have followed me. "No fucking way."

"Way." I walk up the stairs and nudge Casey with my knee. She pushes up off the concrete, giving me room to unlock the door. Shoving my key in the lock, I twist it and push the door open. I turn to Casey before glancing at Connor. She's standing off to the side, her eyes bouncing between me and the sexy Adonis, who looks like he's still trying to figure out what's going on. She dances in place, squeezing her legs together.

"We're gonna talk about this *after* I go pee." She rushes into the house, our front door slamming loudly behind her.

"So," I say, walking toward Connor. "It turns out I have this really hot neighbor. You should probably be jealous."

"Do you walk around naked?" he asks with a cat-ate-the-canary grin. Warm fingers wrap around mine. He tugs on my hand and I fall forward against his big, hard chest.

"Only when my sister isn't home."

"Good to know. Don't tell your neighbor that or he'll be dropping by for unexpected visits. You know"—he shrugs—"to borrow sugar...and stuff."

"Sugar?" I scrunch up my nose. "He doesn't look like the baking type."

Connor tilts his head to the side and brings his mouth to mine. He kisses me long and slow, only pulling away when we're both breathless and fighting for air.

"He is now." Connor winks and slaps my ass playfully before heading in the direction of his door. "He's gonna be baking all the damn time," he says, laughing, as he disappears into his house.

Well played, Connor. Well played.

Chapter 6

Connor

IT'S BEEN THREE DAYS SINCE I LEFT BRITTANY standing on her front porch. I knew the duplex next to mine had sold, but I've been working so much lately I never paid attention to whether or not someone had actually moved in. There's been an old Grand Prix sitting out front a couple of times and a sleek black Audi, but I didn't think much of it. Today, the Grand Prix is gone, but the Audi isn't, and I'm about to find out if the sexy little car belongs to my sexy little neighbor.

Running a finger over my smartphone, it comes to life, and I shoot her a quick text.

Me: Who drives the black Audi?

Her reply is almost instant.

Brittany: Who is this?

Me: It's your really hot neighbor.

Brittany: How did you get my number?

Me: Changed your mind already, huh?

Brittany: Not at all. I was actually wondering when you were going to make your move. Is this you making your move?

And that right there is exactly why I'm so insanely attracted to Brittany. There aren't many women who are willing to speak their minds, but she has no problem with it. Smiling to myself, I type out a quick response.

Me: I actually tried to make my move yesterday. Went over to your place to borrow a cup of sugar, but Casey said you were working. She gave me your number.

Staring at my phone, I wait for her to reply. A couple of minutes pass and then I internally berate myself for waiting on a text. "Fuck no," I mumble to myself.

Flipping on the TV, I find the sports channel and settle in to watch a recap of last night's major league baseball games. The announcers are talking excitedly about the Cardinals win over the Cubs, and as they debate whether or not the Cards will sweep the series in tonight's game, I pull out my wallet to check—for the fifth time—that the tickets are still there.

I'm tucking them away just as a soft tap on the front door catches my attention. I shove my wallet back in my pocket, walk to the front door, and pull it open. Brittany smiles, revealing two of the cutest damn dimples I've ever seen. *How in the world did I miss those before?*

"Borrowing sugar from another woman, huh?" she says, clicking her tongue against the roof of her mouth.

I prop my hip against the doorframe. "Nah, I don't want another woman's sugar."

Brittany's face lights up. "Good answer, Mr. Jackson. You just earned yourself something swee—"

She doesn't get the chance to finish her sentence because I yank her into my house and swallow her words with my mouth.

"Well"—she pulls back and runs a thumb along her bottom lip—"that was more spicy than sweet, but I like spicy."

"Oh yeah?"

"Mmm hmmm." She nods as I lower my mouth to the side of her neck. "I like it a whole lot."

"Go out with me tonight," I whisper.

"Okay," she says, tilting her head to the side. She

brings her hands to my arms and steadies herself. She tastes so damn good; I can't help but nip at her shoulder. "If you keep doing that, I'd probably agree to just about anything."

"Then maybe I'll have to do it again tonight after the baseball game."

"Baseball game?" Brittany squirms and I look up. "Who's going to a baseball game?"

"We are," I say, pulling my wallet out once again. "You did agree to go out with me, didn't you?"

"Yes." I hand her the tickets and her eyes widen. "Connor," she breathes out, looking between me and the two tickets that cost me a small fortune. "These are front row seats."

"I know."

She shakes her head. "Not just any front row seats. They're right behind home plate."

"We should be able to see everything."

Brittany's eyes glisten under the soft light and my gut twists. *Is she crying? Did I do something wrong?*

"I can't believe you did this. How did you..." She snaps her mouth shut, swallows hard, and blinks several times.

I snatch the tickets from her hands. "We don't have to go," I say, desperate to fix whatever the hell I did to make her cry. "We can do something else, like go catch a movie or have dinner or something."

"No." She steals the tickets back. "The game is perfect. It's exactly what I would've picked. It's just that... well... no one has ever done something like this for me before."

I have the intense urge to punch her ex in the nose. What man in his right mind wouldn't want to spoil this woman? I sure as hell do. Especially when she looks at me with those big, expressive doe eyes— like she is right now. "Well, I'm not your normal guy."

"No," she whispers. "You're not."

"So," I say, sliding my hand to her waist. "How fast can you get decked out in your Cardinals gear? I'd like to take you out for lunch before the game."

"No ballpark food?" She pushes her plump bottom lip out and it's too damn enticing. Leaning forward, I suck the offending piece of flesh into my mouth.

"Definitely ballpark food," I say, biting gently on her lower lip. "But a light lunch first."

Brittany pats my chest and steps away. "I'll be back in ten minutes!"

Spinning on her heel, she runs out of my house. And, if I'm not mistaken, she just took a tiny little piece of my heart with her.

Chapter 7

Connor

"CONNOR," SHE SAYS, NUDGING MY ARM. "THIS is amazing. I've never been this close." The look on her face is priceless and tugs at something deep in my chest. Brittany's lips part, a wide smile stretching across her face.

Casey told me her sister has an addiction to the St. Louis Cardinals, but I don't think Casey even knows just how deep that addiction runs. When Brittany showed back up to my house earlier today, she was wearing a red Cardinals shirt with a matching hat and even dangling Cardinals earrings. But the kicker was her shoes. Yes, the girl has Cardinals shoes.

Her blonde hair was pulled up in a ponytail and tucked into her Cardinals hat—an incredibly sexy look on her—and she had her face painted with a red number four proudly displayed across her left cheek.

"Oh my gosh, there's Yadi!"

Who the fuck is Yadi?

My eyes follow her gaze. Sure enough, there he is—number four. Apparently, *Yadi* is the object of my date's affection.

"Have you always been a Cardinals fan?" I ask, genuinely interested.

Dragging her eyes back to mine, she nods. "Yep. My dad is a huge baseball fan. He used to bring me to games all the time, but we sure as hell couldn't afford seats like these. We were usually in the nosebleeds. Way up there," she says, pointing to the top of the stadium. "But that didn't matter. It was our thing."

I wish I had memories like that. Hell, I wish I had a dad. I take that back. I've got a dad—somewhere—but the piece of shit decided drugs were more important than his own kid.

"How about you?" Brittany asks. "How long have you been a fan?"

I tilt my head to the side. "About three days."

"What?" she asks, crinkling her nose.

"I've never been much of a sports fan." I shrug,

leaving out the fact that I didn't even have a TV to watch sports until I was put into foster care at the age of fifteen. And even then I wasn't allowed to actually watch the TV. "When your sister told me how much of a Cardinals fan you were, I decided I should rectify that."

Brittany watches me for what feels like hours, her blue eyes churning with emotion. Warm fingers tangle with mine, and I look down at our joined hands and then back up at her. "I'm not really sure what to say."

Leaning over the arm rail, she kisses me gently on the lips. I don't know what it is, but I'm starting to think she has a magic mouth. Every time we kiss, it's as if nothing else in the world matters but *that* kiss. At first I thought it was just a fluke, but I'll be damned if it doesn't happen every single time.

Brittany pulls back and my mouth follows hers, begging for more. "You're getting major points for this," she says softly.

"Hmm, I like the sound of that."

Brittany glances over my shoulder and her eyes light up. "Cotton candy!"

"What?" I ask, caught off guard by the sudden change of subject.

Standing up, Brittany waves down a vendor loaded down with bags of sugar on a stick. When the young girl reaches our row, Brittany says, "Two bags, please."

"Why two bags?" I ask, pulling out my wallet. No way am I letting her pay for a thing today. Brittany swats at my hand, but I'm taller and my arms are longer. I hand the girl a twenty-dollar bill and she gives me change, along with two bags of cotton candy.

"Because," Brittany says, grabbing the pink one from my hand, leaving me with the blue. "I don't share well and you'll undoubtedly want a bite of mine. This eliminates that problem."

Chuckling, I open up my bag and pull off a chunk. "Well, aren't you a smart cookie?" I say, popping the bite in my mouth.

"I am a doctor, you know." She gives me a smug smile then tosses a bite into her mouth.

My jaw nearly hits the floor. *She's a fucking doctor?* What in the hell would a doctor see in me? I'm not at all ashamed of what I do for a living, and I'm certainly not living paycheck to paycheck, but still... "You're a doctor? How did I not know this?"

Wrapping her lips around her thumb, Brittany sucks the sticky flesh into her mouth. My eyes follow the movement, and my blood starts pumping to places that have no need for it at the moment. Now if we weren't in the middle of a crowded stadium...

I shift in my seat as Brittany slowly drags her

thumb out of her mouth. "Did you like that?" she asks, sounding coy. *The little minx.*

"Hell yes, I like it. Now answer my question."

"I forgot what it was." Her eyes drift to my mouth and I bend my head to capture her gaze.

"I didn't know you were a doctor."

She smiles. "You never asked. Plus, this is only our first date so there are lots of things about me you don't know."

"Tell me something."

"Okay," she says, pushing up from her seat. Looking around, I notice everyone around us is also standing, so I follow suit. "I get a little crazy at Cardinals games."

"Like how crazy?" I ask.

Brittany turns her attention to the field, where the players are starting to take their positions, and starts clapping along with everyone else. "Crazy enough that I feel like I should apologize now for my behavior." She winks, not taking her eyes off the field.

"Come on, you can't be that bad."

Holy shit, she *can* be that bad.

It's the bottom of the fourth inning and the crowd

roars, heckling the umpire. Brittany jumps from her chair and pushes her face against the screen that's separating our seats from the field. "You've gotta be freakin' kidding me!" she yells. "That's the worst call I've seen all year. Did you even see that ball—?"

Spinning around, the umpire glares at Brittany, and I slap a hand over her mouth. She continues to scream, but at least this way it's muffled and won't get us kicked out of the ballpark.

I hope.

I press my lips to her ears. "Shh. You've got to calm down," I say, fighting back laughter. Turns out Brittany is a little spitfire, and I'd be lying if I said it wasn't a huge turn-on.

Wiggling from my hold, she opens her mouth, no doubt to tell me where to shove my words, but she doesn't get a chance. I slam my mouth against hers and push my tongue inside for a searing kiss. Then, just as fast, I pull away.

Brittany stumbles backward, looking a bit stunned.

"Am I forgiven?" I ask, stifling a smile when some-one behind us hollers for us to get a room. Brittany nods and lowers herself into her seat. "Good, because I'd hate to—"

"Strike three!" the umpire yells, signaling an out

for Brittany's boy, Yadi.

Oh shit.

"*What?*" In a split second, she's pressed against the screen.

Again.

"Come on, Blue!" She tosses her hands up in the air. "Are you even paying attention over there? Pull your head outta your ass!"

The bear of a man that was sitting next to Brittany joins her at the netting, mimicking her displeasure, then they high-five each other. The umpire turns around and points a finger at Brittany and her accomplice.

"I've got her," I say, wrapping an arm around her stomach. She struggles when I lift her up and settle her in my lap. At least this way I can keep a firm grip on her. Brittany continues to bounce around, trying to break free, before finally giving up.

I realize in this moment that I won't let her go. Not now—maybe not ever.

"You do know we're winning, right?" I ask.

"That doesn't matter." Brittany crosses her arms over her chest. The movement causes her shirt to rise, revealing a hint of skin above the waistline of her jeans. "It's the principle! That was clearly a ball, which would've been ball *four*, which would've been a walk for Yadi. With the bases loaded, Wainwright would've walked into home and Carpenter was up to bat. Do you know what Carpenter could've done with the bases loaded?"

"No." And to be honest, I don't care. Right now, the only thing I care about is the creamy skin playing peekaboo above Brittany's waistband. My arm is already wrapped around her stomach, so I slip my fingers under the hem of her shirt, praying that she doesn't ram an elbow into my gut. When I stroke the soft skin with my thumb, she shivers but doesn't pull away. "What could Carpenter have done?" I ask.

Glancing over her shoulder, Brittany looks at me and furrows her brow. "Huh?"

I chuckle and bury my face in her back. She's so damn cute. "You asked me if I knew what Carpenter could do with the bases loaded."

"I did? Oh, right, I did." She shakes her head and turns back around, mumbling something that sounds an awful lot like *'I can't think straight when you touch me.'*

"What was that?" I ask, wanting to make sure I heard her right. She may not like that she can't think straight when I touch her, but I sure as hell do.

"Nothing." She sighs. "I didn't say anything."

The next few innings go by without incident. All

too soon it's the seventh inning and everyone is, in fact, standing to stretch. Pressing my lips to Brittany's neck, I whisper, "I'm proud of you. You went three innings without calling the umpire an asshole *or* a jackass."

"Thank you," she says. I loosen my hold around her waist and we stand up. Puffing out her chest, Brittany raises her arms and stretches like a cat. "I feel like I deserve some sort of prize or something."

"A prize, huh?" Funny, because being here with Brittany, I feel like I *won* some sort of prize.

She nods.

Grabbing my beer from the cup holder, I tilt my head back and take a swig. "Name it and it's yours."

She smiles like the Cheshire Cat. "Anything?"

"Anything." I'm secretly hoping that whatever she asks for involves the two of us getting naked.

"Nachos," she states firmly. *Nachos?*

"I said you can have anything you want, and you choose nachos?"

Tossing her head back, Brittany lets out a deep, throaty laugh that travels straight to my dick, stroking it several times. This woman is going to be the death of me. No woman's laugh should be able to make a man feel *that*.

"But I'm hungry," she says, slipping her hand in mine. I follow behind her as she leads us toward the main aisle then weaves through the crowd, presumably in search of a food stand. "How can you be hungry? You had lunch, cotton candy, a jumbo hot dog, and half of my pretzel."

"What can I say?" She shrugs, not stopping in her quest for nachos. "I love ballpark food."

Chapter 8

Brittany

"Connor?" My stomach rolls, and when he doesn't answer or look at me, I tap his arm. "Connor?"

The crowd goes wild and it pains me to say I have absolutely no idea what just happened. Connor jumps up, fist pumping the air, and despite my ever-growing nausea, I love that he's enjoying the game.

I nudge him one more time. "Connor?"

"Sorry. That was intense," he says excitedly. Dropping onto his seat, he looks over at me, and immediately his brows dip low. "Are you okay?" he asks, pressing the back of his hand against my forehead. "You don't look so good."

Closing my eyes, I swallow past the burning in my throat. "I hate ballpark food," I grumble.

"Shit," he hisses, and suddenly the empty nacho tray is no longer in my hands. I open my eyes to see Connor looking around us frantically. "Are you going to get sick? Do they have barf bags around here somewhere?"

"No." I start to chuckle but my stomach clenches tight, so I bend over in pain instead. "Can we go home?"

"Yes," he says, grabbing at my purse and foam finger, which I insisted on buying earlier. "Can you walk or do I need to carry you?"

"I can walk." Ever so slowly, I stand up and follow Connor to the aisle. As we start up the stairs, he wraps an arm around my shoulders, bearing the majority of my weight. My stomach churns with each step we take toward the stadium's exit. When warm saliva fills my mouth, I run for the nearest trashcan and bend over as my stomach heaves. Pain rips up my throat as I lose every single thing I ate today.

A warm hand lands on my back and begins rubbing big, slow circles. Connor uses his other hand to hold my ponytail out of the way. He doesn't move or say a word, but he doesn't have to. His actions today speak so much louder than words. Tears burn my eyes at his kind gesture, making me grateful that I have the throwing up to mask my sudden emotional response.

My stomach finally settles. Straightening my back, I offer Connor a sad smile. He searches my face for a second before draping the strap of my purse over his shoulder. He pulls the foam finger from under his arm, hands it to me, and then scoops me up. "I don't like seeing you sick," he mumbles, taking off toward the car.

"I can walk," I say meekly. Dropping my head to his shoulder, I silently pray that he doesn't put me down.

"I know you can." Connor tightens his hold on me. I may not feel the best, but I'm still able to appreciate his big, strong arms wrapped around me. It's nice being taken care of for a change.

And for the first time in a long time, I feel safe and content in the arms of a man. It's as if I saw him in the tattoo parlor and my heart said, *'oh, there you are.'* That's a scary thought considering this is our first official date, so I try not to dwell on it and just enjoy the simplicity of the moment.

"Come on, pretty girl," Connor says, gently retrieving me from the front seat of his car. My eyes fly open as he cradles me against his chest.

"Did I fall asleep?" I ask, stifling a yawn.

"Yep, and just so you know, you snore." Connor kisses the side of my head. I squirm to get down, but he doesn't relent. "It's okay, I found it kind of cute."

"I don't snore," I scoff, wiggling again. "Do you have a thing for holding women or what?"

"Not women," he says, walking toward my door. "Just you. It turns out I have a thing for holding *you*. Don't ask me," he says, shrugging. "I can't figure it out either."

Damn he's good.

So, so good.

The front door flies open as soon as we hit the welcome mat. Casey shakes her head, making a *tsking* sound. "I've been waiting for you."

"You have?" Connor asks, sounding confused.

"Yep," she says, popping the *P*. "She does this *every single* time. The woman doesn't know when to stop. Actually," she says, motioning for Connor to walk inside, "I'm thinking of finding some sort of ballpark food addiction group she can join."

Connor sets me on my feet but keeps a hand settled on my lower back. "Ha, ha. Very funny." Plopping down on the couch, I glare at Casey. "Now, quit making fun of the sick girl. It isn't nice."

Casey purses her lips, failing miserably at trying to hide her smile. "You aren't sick, you just ate too much. Big difference."

I roll my eyes and Connor laughs. "You did eat a ton." Sticking my bottom lip out, I give him my best pouty look. He bends down and kisses my forehead. "Want me to stay for a while?" he whispers, his eyes flitting to Casey and then back to me.

"No." I groan. Grabbing the afghan off the back of the couch, I drape it over myself. "She's right, this happens all the time. I'll be miserable for a few hours, but I'll be okay. No sense in you hanging around. Plus, it's getting late."

"Are you sure? I really don't mind," he says, tucking the edges of the blanket around my shoulders.

The gesture is so damn sweet it makes my teeth ache. Fisting my hand in the front of his shirt, I pull him toward me. "If I didn't have vomit breath, I'd kiss the hell out of you right now."

Connor flashes me his pearly whites. "Oh yeah? Can I get a rain check?"

"I'll give you something better than a rain check."

"Oh, good Lord." Casey huffs and walks out of the room. "Now *I'm* going to vomit."

Connor and I both laugh, keeping our gazes locked on each other. "Thank you for today," I tell him sincerely. "It was the best first date in the history of first dates."

"I'm glad you had fun. Next time I'll know to limit your consumption of food though." Connor bends down a little bit lower. Instinctively, I pull back because I really do have rank breath. "And just so you're prepared, the next time I'm leaning over you on a couch, it'll be for completely different reasons."

If I had been standing, I would've fallen, because Connor's mention of 'next time' made my knees go weak. And now I *really* want to know what those 'different reasons' will be. "Are you busy tomorrow night?"

"No." Connor grins. "But even if I was, I'd break my plans." He kisses my forehead once more before heading out the door.

"Where's he going?" Casey asks, walking back into the room.

"Home." Rolling over, I curl in a ball, doing my best to calm the tornado swirling around inside my stomach.

Casey stops in front of me and holds out her hand. "I thought some Tums might make you feel better."

"Thanks." I take the two pink tablets from my sister and chew them up.

Casey sits in the recliner next to the couch. "So, other than you eating way too much food and making yourself sick, how was your date?"

"It was really great."

"Wow," she says, pulling one of her legs to her chest. "Not just great, but *really great*." I swallow hard and Casey quickly sits up. "Are you going to get sick?"

"No." Closing my eyes, I shake my head. "I already did that. In front of Connor. Not my finest moment, let me tell ya."

"Oh shit," she says, laughing. Opening my eyes, I pin her with a glare. "What? It was your own fault. You've been doing it for years. You should know when to stop by now."

"I know," I grumble. The insane amount of fullness I felt in my stomach earlier finally starts to subside, and I feel like I can actually breathe again. "I'll try not to screw things up next time."

"Will there be a next time?"

Taking a deep breath, I let it out slowly. "Yes." Casey's eyes widen. Even I'm surprised at how easily that word fell from my lips. The past two years haven't been easy for me, and actually going out on a date—let alone agreeing to a second one—is huge.

"Good." The smile on Casey's face is genuine. "I'm happy for you. If anyone deserves to be happy, it's you.

Just promise me something."

"What?" I ask skeptically.

"Promise me that you'll be honest. Whatever your feelings, good or bad, just be honest. Don't run away from them."

It's really quite scary how well she knows me.

I blink several times, pulling my bottom lip in between my teeth. Casey cocks her head to the side, waiting for me to consent. "I promise."

"Good." She pushes up from the chair. "Do you need anything? Because I think I'm going to hit the sack."

"No, I'm good. I'm just going to lie here until my stomach feels better, and then I'm going to go to bed too."

"Good night." Casey turns toward the hall, but I stop her before she can get too far.

"Hey, Case?"

She spins around, covering a yawn with her hand. "Yeah?"

"Thank you."

"For what?"

"For tipping him off about my love for the Cardinals. I still can't believe he got us front row seats."

Casey puffs out her chest. "Well, I can't take credit for the front row seats, but I'll definitely take credit for clueing him in. You can pay me back by naming your firstborn child after me."

"Yeah, right. One of you in my life is enough."

"Whatever." Twisting around, she flings her long, dark hair over her shoulder. "I'm fabulous and you know it."

Casey disappears around the corner and I close my eyes, deciding that maybe some sleep is the best thing for me right now. Only when I close my eyes, sleep doesn't come. Instead, all I see is Connor and his big chiseled body covering my own.

Screw it, who needs sleep anyway.

Chapter 9

Brittany

THE CLOCK DINGS—*AGAIN*—AND I SILENTLY berate my mother for giving me the damn thing. Don't get me wrong, I love the antique clock. It was passed down from my grandmother to my mother, and then to me. But right now it's pissing me the hell off. According to my family heirloom, it's now two o'clock in the morning and I've spent the last four hours thinking. And for me, thinking isn't good, because I tend to overthink, which is exactly what I've done tonight. Connor's laugh, his smile, his touch— he's consuming me. I'm finding myself obsessing over what it would be like to become attached to all of those things, only to have them ripped away. Honestly, I'm not sure I could handle going through something like that again. Then again, he wouldn't do that to me… but he could.

What the hell is wrong with me?

Flinging my legs over the edge of the couch, I rub absently at my heavy lids. Connor's told me that he doesn't do meaningless sex, but he never said he does long-term relationships either.

Shit.

My own thoughts cause my breath to hitch in my throat. What if I'm ready to give up my rogue ways at the chance for something more but Connor changed his mind? What if he saw my brand of crazy tonight and decided to cut his losses and run?

Adrenaline pumps through veins, my body vibrating with uncertainty. The need to see him—to talk to him—is overwhelming, and before I know what's happening, I'm heading toward the door. Thank God he lives close.

Scurrying across the yard, I hop up the steps. His lights are off. Biting nervously at my lip, I try to decide whether or not I should just turn around.

This is crazy.

Running a hand through my hair, I spin around to head back home. I make it two steps and then Casey's words slam into me like a freight train. *Promise me that you'll be honest. Whatever your feelings, good or bad, just be honest. Don't run away from them.*

Damn it. She's right. I hate it when she's right.

If I go home now, I'll most likely talk myself out of whatever this is with Connor. And I really, *really* don't want to do that.

Twirling back around, I take two measured steps, along with a deep breath. I tap the door lightly and then step back. My stomach is twisting in knots, and this time it has nothing to do with my overindulgence of ballpark food and everything to do with Connor.

A couple of seconds pass with no answer. I knock again, a little bit louder this time, and turn around to double-check that his car is still in the driveway. Just then the door flings open, and the sight in front of me causes my heart to go from a steady trot to a full-on gallop.

Connor rubs lazily at his sleep-ridden eyes. His shirt is gone, leaving me with the ridiculously sexy view of his defined stomach, that perfect little V I had so much fun with the other night, and lines upon lines of a tattoo that I want to examine more closely. Shorts hang low on his hips and my eyes are drawn to his erection straining against the gauzy material.

Interesting. I thought men got morning wood. I

guess, technically, it is the morning.

Connor clears his throat. "Are you okay?" he asks.

My lady bits tingle at the sound of his scratchy voice and I glance up, meeting his gaze. He looks so rumpled, and a tiny piece of me feels bad for waking him up.

I shake my head. "No." Connor's droopy eyelids open wide and he yanks me into his house. He pushes the door shut behind me and then large, warm hands roam over my body. It takes me a second to realize what he's doing. Chuckling, I pull back. "Yes. I mean, yes. Physically, I'm okay."

"Thank God." Connor sighs, pressing a hand to the center of his chest. "I hated leaving you earlier, and I thought about you for hours before I finally fell asleep."

His words knock the breath right out of me. My heart swells inside my chest, clogging my throat. Swallowing hard, I push past the rush of emotions. "You did?"

"Yes." He runs a hand through his shaggy hair. "And then you show up and tell me that you're not okay. You scared the hell out of me there for a second."

"I'm sorry," I say quietly, trying to find the words for what I really want to say—for what brought me to his door in the middle of the night. Sucking my bot-

tom lip into my mouth, I look down at my sock-cov-
ered feet.

Connor takes a step forward and his bare feet
come into view. Placing a finger under my chin, he
tilts my face upward and our eyes meet. "What's going
on?" he asks, concern filling his voice.

He lowers his hand, and I catch it on the way down,
entwining our fingers. His thumb rubs along the palm
of my hand, quickly putting me at ease. "Please tell me
you feel this," I say, my words rushing out. "Because I
feel it. I can't explain it, but it terrifies me." I continue,
leaving out *why* it terrifies me, because it feels good to
get it out. "And I'd feel a whole heck of a lot better if I
knew you felt it, too."

Cupping my face in his hands, Connor pulls me
in close. His sweet breath fans across my cheeks. "I feel
it, too," he whispers, his big blue eyes flitting between
mine. "But why are you scared?"

"I'm not a long-term kind of girl," I blurt. My eyes
fill with tears, but I quickly blink them away. "I'm not
even a right now kind of girl."

Connor grins. "Then what kind of girl are you?"

"I have no freaking clue."

Brushing his thumb along my bottom lip, Connor
searches my face. "You've been hurt." I'm not sure if
he's stating a fact or asking me a question, but I nod

anyway. One of those pesky tears that had been threatening to break free finally does, and Connor catches it with his thumb. "Let me tell you what I think," he says, holding my gaze. "You've been burned one too many times. Shutting yourself off was easier than trying again, and now you're scared."

My throat feels thick. The familiar burning in my nose signals an onslaught of tears. Despite my best attempt, I'm unable to hold them in any longer.

"Here's the thing." He swipes a finger under my eyes before continuing. "Whoever hurt you is a prick. He has absolutely no idea what he lost or gave up. But I *see* you," he says, bringing my face even closer. "You're incredibly strong, independent, funny, and tenacious. I adore all of those things about you. But you've also got this gentle side that I think most people don't see, and *that's* what I want to explore."

Soft lips descend on mine before moving from one cheek to the other as he kisses away my tears. With each press of his lips against my skin, the shattered pieces of my heart are slowly put back together. I realize some of the edges may be jagged and it'll take time to smooth them out, but I'm hopeful this man will be the one to do it.

"I can assure you that if you step out of the box you've holed yourself up in, you won't regret it. This chemistry between us," he says, waving a hand between our bodies, "is nothing I've ever felt before. I have no idea what it means or what all of this will amount to, but I want to find out." Connor drops his forehead to mine. "I promise you that I won't hurt you."

"I'm not worried that you'll hurt me." My voice is shaky. Taking a deep breath, I try to regain some sort of composure.

Connor furrows his brow. "Then what are you worried about?"

"That I'll hurt *you*." Lifting my hands, I wrap my fingers around each of Connor's wrists.

"How about you let me worry about that."

"But—"

"Nope." Connor presses a finger to my lips. "You already told me you were giving this a chance, and I'm holding you to it. This *is* happening."

I sigh and Connor drops his finger from my mouth. "Okay," I breathe, giving him control.

Connor's smile is blinding. "Okay."

Chapter 10

Connor

THIS GIRL.

She fucking kills me.

Grabbing Brittany's hand, I lead her toward my bedroom. Thank God she follows behind without question, because there is no way in hell I'd be able to let her go tonight. Pulling back the covers of what has always been the empty side of my bed, I motion for her to climb in.

"Umm…with my clothes on?" she asks, looking a little unsure.

"Yes," I say, chuckling. "With your clothes on."

She slips between the covers like a good girl. I

pull them up to her chest, then walk around the bed, and slide in next to her. Situating the pillow under my head, I lie on my back.

"Come here," I say, holding out my arm. She doesn't hesitate. Her lithe body cuddles up next to mine. Curling herself into the crook of my arm, she rests her head on my chest. I tangle my fingers with hers and bring her arm across my stomach. *Perfect.*

"What's your favorite color?"

Propping her chin on my chest, she examines me. "You brought me to bed so you could ask me what my favorite color is?"

"Oh no," I counter. "I also want to know how you take your coffee in the morning, what your favorite food is, what types of books you prefer, your favorite childhood memory, where your other tattoo is... The list goes on and on, so we could be up all night if you don't cooperate."

Brittany's eyes twinkle with what I can only describe as pure happiness. "Okay." She nods, resting her head back down on my chest. "Purple. I don't drink coffee. Pizza, but it has to be Chicago style. Romance. Cuddling with my mom at night. And," she says, dragging the word out, "you'll have to find it yourself."

"Wow." I laugh, amazed she remembered the order in which I said everything. "I'm impressed. And trust me"—bringing her hand to my lips, I pepper kisses across her knuckles—"I have every intention of finding that tattoo."

She doesn't look up, but I feel her smile against my skin. "What about you? Same questions," she says.

"Hmmm." Closing my eyes, I try to remember everything I asked her. "Red. Black with one scoop of sugar. Lasagna. Thrillers, but I'm open to this 'romance' that you speak of as long as we get to try out what we read." A burst of laughter rips from Brittany's chest. The exact reaction I was hoping for. "Listening to music with my best friend, Logan. Also, I have a ton of tattoos you're more than welcome to explore any time you please."

I open my eyes to find Brittany watching me. "Your favorite childhood memory is of listening to music with your best friend?"

Shit.

"It is." I take a deep breath, preparing myself for what I suspect will be her next question.

"What's your favorite memory of your parents or your family? Speaking of family, do you have any brothers or sisters?"

And there it is.

"The majority of my childhood memories involving my parents aren't good."

Brittany's eyes soften, but she isn't looking at me with pity. "I'm sorry to hear that." She looks across the room, worrying her bottom lip between her teeth.

"What is it?" I already know what she wants to ask; it's the same thing everybody else wants to ask. People always want to know why my childhood was shitty. They want the nitty-gritty details. I'm not ashamed of my past—I've worked too damn hard to move away from it—but I also don't necessarily like talking about it. To other people, that is. For some reason, I want Brittany to ask me. I want her to know.

"Is it too soon for me to ask what happened?"

"You can ask me anything you want." The words don't surprise me. With her, I seem to be an open book. "My parents were druggies. Mom ran out on us when I was six. I don't really remember a whole lot about her, and the few memories I do recall aren't pleasant."

"Like what?" Brittany asks.

"Well, I remember seeing her falling over and stumbling around the house. At the time, I didn't understand. I know now that she was most likely either drunk or high. And I remember my dad smacking her around a few times, but that's about it."

Brittany pulls her hand from mine. Resting it against my chest, she starts drawing slow circles with the tip of her finger. "What happened after she left?"

"My dad got worse. He was drunk or high nearly all the time. Eventually, he lost his job, which resulted in us losing our house. That's actually how I got taken away from him. One of my teachers found out we were living in his car. And you know what?" Brittany raises her eyebrows but doesn't say a word, and I'm grateful because it feels good to tell her this. Other than my foster siblings, I've never told anyone about my childhood. "He didn't seem to care. I think he was just glad to get rid of me."

"Wow," she says, sighing heavily. "I don't know what to say."

"You don't have to say anything," I whisper, running a hand through her hair.

"What happened after that?"

"I was put into foster care. Moved from house to house until I ended up at the Smiths' when I was sixteen. That's where I met Logan. In fact, that's also where I met Isabelle, Ryan, Jake, and Carter."

"Your foster brothers and sisters?"

I nod. "Logan and I were closest in age, so our friendship was almost instantaneous. In fact, we're still best friends, and we see each other nearly every day. Isabelle was younger so we weren't as close, and I haven't seen her in years. Ryan and Jake are biological brothers, and we've stayed in contact over the years.

Carter..." A sharp pain rips through my chest and I take a moment to collect my thoughts before continuing. "He, um...he battled with depression most of his life. He committed suicide three years ago."

Brittany's eyes go wide. "Oh my gosh," she says, her grip on my body tightening. "I'm so sorry."

"Yeah, not gonna lie, that was hard for Logan and me. Carter was like our big brother. Shit, he *was* our big brother. When we turned eighteen and got released from the system, it was Carter that was there to help us out." My eyes drift across the room, landing on the picture of the two of us that sits on my dresser. "He helped us enroll in college, gave us a place to live, and when we started down a bad path, he was the one to bring us back. I owe him my life."

"He sounds like a great guy. I'm glad you had someone like him."

"Me, too," I say, bringing my eyes back to Brittany. "If it weren't for him, I wouldn't be doing what I love."

"Was he a tattoo artist?" she asks.

"He was. That's how I ended up at InkSlingers."

Brittany's lips part, understanding flashing across her face. "I was wondering about that," she says.

"About what?"

"Well, I remember seeing you on *Inked*. You won a decent chunk of money to start up your own parlor, but instead you work out of InkSlingers. But it was his, wasn't it? It was Carter's shop."

"It was," I say. "When Carter died, he left the shop to me—"

"Not to Logan?" she asks, interrupting me.

"Nope. Logan never had anything to do with the shop. I was Carter's apprentice, and he taught me everything I know. Anyway, the first year after he left me the shop was tough. I was on the brink of foreclosure when Logan suggested I try out for *Inked,* and, well, the rest is history. I put a big chunk of money into the business, paying off debts, updating equipment, all that good stuff. And I'm glad I did. That parlor is my life, and I want to make it as successful as possible."

"I love that." Our eyes stay locked for several seconds. Out of nowhere, she leans forward, presses her warm lips to the center of my chest, and then wraps herself around me. "You amaze me, Connor Jackson. I feel like you're too good to be true. Like one of those sexy men I read about in my romance novels."

"Oooh," I say, rubbing my hand along the top of her head. I thread my fingers into her blonde hair and let the strands slowly fall where they may. "I like where this is going. Does the sexy man end up with the girl?"

She giggles. The tinkling sound radiates through my body before settling in the center of my chest. "I guess you'll have to start reading some books to find out."

"Well played, Dr. Caldwell. Well played."

Brittany's head pops up. "You know my last name?" Her lips tilt, revealing those beautiful white teeth. "That sounded so bad. I'm in bed with a man that I didn't think knew my last name. In fact," she says, furrowing her brows, "how *did* you know my last name?"

"I'm psychic."

"Yeah, right." She slaps playfully at my chest. "Tell me."

"You were in my appointment book, remember? I knew who you were the second I walked into my shop that day."

"Oh." She nuzzles her face back into my chest. "I didn't think about that."

"But I didn't know you were a doctor, which is pretty awesome. What type of practice do you work in?"

Brittany yawns as I continue stroking my fingers through her hair. "I work in the ER."

"Wow, that must be intense." I can't imagine the types of things she's witnessed.

"It has its days. When I lived in New York, I worked in a trauma ER. Now *that* was intense. It almost makes the ER here seem easy."

"But you like it? You're happy?"

"I am. Taking care of people is what I've always wanted to do. And not only do I take care of people, but I save lives. I wouldn't change it for the world."

I drop a kiss to the top of her head. "I think you're the amazing one."

"Mmmm..."

A couple of minutes pass, the silence even more comforting than I had predicted. Brittany's breathing evens out, and when I'm certain she's asleep, I close my eyes.

It's been years since I've actually slept with a woman, and even then it didn't feel like *this*. It probably makes me sound like a fucking pussy, but as long as our bodies are touching in some way, everything in the world just feels right.

Chapter 11

Brittany

PULLING THE COVERS BACK, I TAKE IN THE yumminess that is Connor's body. It's magnificent in every way...perfection at its absolute finest. The sheet is bunched around his hips, giving me a perfect view of all of his intricate tattoos. I have every intention of exploring them individually, but right now I'm transfixed on his body. From the waist up, he's all smooth lines and chiseled curves. It's the type of body women dream of, the type that only exists in books and on TV. Except this isn't a book and we sure as hell aren't on TV—this is my life, Connor is real, and as long as I keep playing my cards right, he'll be mine.

My finger traces a slow path from his beard-
ed square jaw down to the base of his neck. I place
a soft kiss against his chin and my eyelids drift shut
as I remember the way the scruff on his face rubbed
against my chest when he worshiped my breasts the
other night. The feeling alone was so damn erotic that
I nearly buried my fingers in his hair and begged him
to stay there forever.

My heavy lids open and I peek up at Connor. He
looks so peaceful when he's sleeping. His dark lashes
are fanned out on his cheek and his lips are pursed in
the sexiest little pout. More than anything, I want to
kiss him awake and demand he make love to me, but
I'm still exploring.

I trail my finger down his chest, stopping at his
heart. Then my lips take over and I kiss his chest several times. Resting the palm of my hand over his left
pec, I make a silent promise to cherish and protect his
heart if he does the same for mine. I know we still have
so much to learn about each other, but I'm ready to
take that next step.

Connor shifts in bed, cocking his leg out to the
side, but he doesn't wake up. His breathing is slow and
steady, making me wonder how far I can go before
he'll stir. I scatter slow, open-mouthed kisses down the

hard plane of his stomach, pausing to trace the etched V that leads to the place I so desperately want to be.

The other night I drove him crazy, and now I'm ready to do it again. That tiny slice of heaven wasn't nearly enough. I want more. I want all of him. I want him so fucking turned on he can't see straight. I want to hear my name falling from his lips when he finally lets go.

Slipping my hand into his shorts, I find him swollen and semi-hard. I move a little lower to get a better angle—

"Brittany." My eyes snap up to his. Connor blinks several times. He looks conflicted, and I can't tell if I'm pushing things too far or if he's desperately trying to refrain from pouncing all over me. It's a toss-up, but I'm hoping for the latter.

"I want you," I whisper, attempting to convey in those three little words just how much I need him. That must have been exactly what he was hoping to hear because, in the blink of an eye, our positions are switched. Connor is hovering over me, his delicious body pressing me into the mattress.

"I want you, too," he says, brushing a strand of hair away from my face. "So much." My body is vibrating with sexual energy, and without thinking, I tilt my hips, silently begging for him to take me. Connor sucks in a sharp breath. Gripping my hips, he grinds against me. "No." Running his thumb along my bottom lip, he shakes his head. "This time, *I'm* controlling the pace."

Sitting back on his haunches, Connor slips his fingers under my shirt and slides it up my body. I lift my upper body just enough for him to pull it off. He flicks the clasp of my bra and the cotton material falls from my heavy breasts. His eyes flare at the sight of my naked chest. "So fucking sexy," he rasps, tugging my bra off. He kisses the swell of each breast. "I've been dying to get my mouth on you again—and I will—but first…" Connor's words trail off. His eyes drop, and then he slowly peels my pants off, along with my underwear.

My eyes stay locked on his. Watching him watch me is the most intense sensation ever. I didn't think it was possible to be more turned on than I was just seconds ago.

I was wrong.

Running his hands from my knees to my ankles, Connor lifts both of my legs, opening them in the process. He kisses one calf and then lowers my leg before repeating the process with the other.

My knees are bent and I'm completely open to him, feeling sexier now than I ever have. "Please," I beg. Lifting my hips, I urge him to touch me.

"No begging," he says. Then he gives me exactly what I want. One long finger pushes inside of me and my eyes roll back in my head. "I'll give you whatever you want." Connor shifts lower on the bed and I peel my eyes open, a little shocked at his admission. "Haven't you figured that out yet? I can't get enough of you." His lips trail along the inside of my thigh, his eyes trained on his finger as it slides in and out of me. His mouth is close enough to join in the torture, but it doesn't.

"Are you watching?" he asks, not taking his eyes off my pussy long enough to check for himself.

Hell yes, I'm watching.

The moment is way too sensual and I can't seem to form words. Connor adds a second finger, pushing it deep inside of me. When he curls them both in a come-hither motion, my body coils tight. "I bet I could make you come just like this. You don't even need my mouth," he says, his voice thick and heady.

He's a dirty talker.

Oh, God. That's my weakness.

"What do you think?" he asks. Pulling his fingers out, he twists his wrist and pushes his fingers back in, only this time with a bit more force.

"Connor." I know, it's not the most clever thing to

say, but right now my brain is mush. The only thing I can concentrate on are his fingers and the way they're hitting that swollen spot way down deep. "Please."

"What did I say, pretty girl? No begging. What do you want? Tell me and it's yours."

I squirm beneath him, pumping my hips in rhythm with his hand. Tiny sparks of pleasure shoot through my body. Tossing my head back, I squeeze my eyes shut. "More. I need more."

"More of what?" he growls. "Tell me what you need."

"Your mouth. I need your—*Oh, God.* That. That's what I—*ahhh*." Connor's tongue pushes inside me at the same time I thread my fingers in his hair and hold him against me. His tongue swirls and lips suck, and when he slides a finger through my wet folds, finding my clit, I nearly lose it.

Connor glances up at me under thick, dark lashes. "Gorgeous," he mumbles. Wrapping his lips around my clit, he sucks—hard—before nipping at the swollen bud. And that's all it takes.

My body spirals out of control, my thighs clenching tightly around his head. Connor's glorious mouth doesn't stop. Instead, he rides out the orgasm, licking and sucking relentlessly until I'm nothing but a big pile of loose limbs.

"I don't even have words for that." Dropping my head back on the pillow, I revel in the feel of Connor's body as he crawls on top of me.

"Open your eyes." It's a gentle command, and one that I'm more than happy to follow. When I lift my lids, Connor's face is mere inches from mine. His mouth is glistening, a lazy smile stretched across his face. "There aren't words for *that*. Watching you come, watching you lose control...it was the sexiest thing I've ever witnessed. I want to see it again," he whispers, then presses a kiss to my lips before sitting up.

Leaning across the bed, Connor grabs a condom from his nightstand. He rips open the foil, pulls out the condom, and slides it over his throbbing erection. As he lowers himself on top of me, he asks, "Do you want this?"

Is that a real question? "Yes."

"Say it," he says, his eyes imploring mine. "I want to hear the words." Connor squeezes a hand between our bodies. His fingers find my clit, which is still swollen and throbbing, and my hips buck off the bed. Then he grinds against me, his erection sliding between my folds. Rocking his hips, Connor slowly pulls my body from its sated state. In a matter of seconds he has me writhing against him, desperate for a second release, and even more desperate to feel him inside me.

"I want you." My throat is dry from panting and my words come out scratchy. Gliding a hand down his back, I squeeze Connor's ass.

Dropping his face to the crook of my neck, he finds my ear. "Do you feel how hard I am? That's all you. Do you want my cock inside you?"

"Yes."

"Be sure, baby. Because once I'm inside you, I'm going to claim you. Your body"—grazing a hand over my breast, he plucks at my nipple—"will be mine. This pussy"—pulling back, he aligns himself at my entrance—"will be mine. Is that what you want?"

The head of his cock slips inside of me. "Yes." The word isn't even out of my mouth and he buries himself to the hilt, filling me in ways that I've never experienced. All of my insecurities fade away. The only thing that matters in this moment is *this* man.

"Fuck." Connor grunts, trailing hot kisses over my chest as he starts moving his body. "You feel so good. I'm not going to last." His hips are pumping in a perfect rhythm, and I meet him thrust for thrust. But I still need more.

Wrapping my legs around his back, I lock my ankles. "Harder." He's pounding into me, each pump pushing him deeper and deeper until I'm certain he's found a permanent spot to call his own. My legs begin to shake. Tightening my thighs around him, I try to hold off my release, wanting to prolong this moment—this feeling—as long as I possibly can. "Connor."

A low rumble emanates from his chest. Wiggling my hand between us, I make a V with my fingers and slide them along my pussy. Then my fingers squeeze his cock as he thrusts in and out of me. "Son of a bitch," he growls, staring at where we're joined.

"Fuck me, Connor," I command in a completely non-commanding voice. Connor's eyes snap up to mine. His hooded gaze is full of desire, showing me he needs this as much as I do. Warmth settles low in my belly. My clit throbs with each smack of his hips against mine, and without warning, my body explodes, sending sparks of pleasure throughout.

Connor's movements become quicker, almost frenzied. A string of unintelligible words tumble from his mouth, and his muscles tighten under the touch of my hands. Within seconds, he's groaning my name as he rides out his own release.

Collapsing on top of me, Connor cradles my face in his hand. "There aren't words for that either," he says.

"I disagree." Curving my hand around the back of his neck, I pull him down until his lips rest against mine. "It was mind-blowing, and I want to do it over and over and over—"

Sealing his mouth against mine, Connor swallows my words. It's the best feeling to have a guy kiss you as though you're the only woman in the world. And that's exactly how I feel every time I'm with this man.

Nibbling on my bottom lip, he slowly pulls back. "You're mind-blowing," he says, peppering kisses anywhere and everywhere he can find a place to kiss. My heart swells painfully inside my chest.

I'm actually beginning to wonder if my broken heart was ever really broken to begin with. Because what I feel for Connor in just a few shorts days is so much more than I ever felt for Tyson. Maybe he isn't piecing my heart back together at all, maybe Connor is stealing my heart one little chunk at a time.

I smile to myself when his lips lock around my nipple. "Is it too soon to do the 'over and over and over again' you were talking about?" he mumbles.

Arching my back, I offer him every bit of my body...and quite possibly my heart. "Absolutely not," I say. "In fact, the sooner the better. What are you waiting for?"

In the blink of an eye, my body is flying through the air as Connor flips me over. Wrapping an arm around my stomach, he pulls me up onto all fours and smacks my ass.

I suck in a sharp breath and arch my back. The sting of his skin slapping mine isn't at all what I expected. It doesn't hurt, and surprisingly I want more. Wiggling my ass, I urge him to do it again.

"Of course you like that," he murmurs, giving me what I want. Connor's hand swiftly connects with my ass again, and then he rubs the area gently before sliding his hand up my back. His fingers skate across the base of my neck, sweeping my hair to the side, and then his touch falters.

"*Alis volat propriis,*" he whispers.

"You found it." My words come out husky and breathless. I'm anxious to get this out of the way so we can get back to that ass smacking.

"What does it mean?"

"She flies with her own wings."

"It's beautiful. I love it."

"Thank you," I say, pushing my ass into his groin, hoping he gets the hint.

"You're going to be the death of me," he breathes, fisting his hand in my hair.

Connor tugs gently, tilting my head back, and a tiny whimper falls from my mouth. Whatever game we've been playing, Connor just won.

Chapter 12

Connor

"WHERE DO YOU THINK YOU'RE GOING?" Tightening my grip on Brittany, I pull her warm, naked body against mine. Her tight little ass pushes against my cock. My body is sated to the point of blissful relaxation and there is no way I'm getting hard again. Although I'm half tempted to see if she'd let me try.

Brittany chuckles, allowing her body to melt into mine. She's all soft curves and silky smooth skin, and I could touch her forever. "Don't you have to work today?" she asks.

"Yes." I kiss the soft spot under her ear. Her shoulders scrunch up, a wave of goose bumps popping out along her skin. I fucking love that I can do that to her.

"My first client doesn't come in until noon. So we still have"—craning my neck, I look at the clock—"two hours."

"I wish," she says, rolling over. "I promised I'd have brunch with my mom."

"Brunch? Do people really have brunch?"

"Yes," she says, shoving playfully at my chest. "Well, I think they do." She furrows her brow. "Or maybe just my mom and I do. Anyway, I'm supposed to meet her at ten-thirty, and I really should get home and shower beforehand."

I smirk. "What, you don't want to go with that fresh I-just-had-the-best-sex-of-my-life look?"

"No," she says, laughing. "As far as I'm concerned, my mother can keep believing I'm a virgin."

"Riiiiight." Trailing my lips down her neck, I suck lightly. "Maybe I should leave you with a parting gift?"

Brittany springs from the bed so fast I don't even have time to react. "Oh hell no," she says, holding her hands out.

Seriously? Like that could stop me. But it's cute that she thinks it could. Sweeping my eyes down her naked body, I take a moment to stare at her.

She glances down as though she just realized she's

in her birthday suit. "Crap," she hisses, covering her gorgeous tits with her arm. Bending down, she looks around, presumably for her clothes.

Flinging the sheet off, I climb out of bed, tug her arm away from her chest, and haul her in close. "Don't hide from me," I say, running my fingertips along her chest. Her eyes drift down, watching my hand as I brush my fingers across the swell of each breast. "Not after what we just did." Placing a finger under her chin, I lift her face to meet mine. "Your body is perfect. I should know, since I just spent hours worshiping every single inch of it. In fact, what are your plans for tonight? Because there are a few spots I'd like to examine a little closer."

Brittany shivers, a light flush infusing her cheeks. I can't help but wonder what it would take to make her flush like that all over. I think I have an idea, but it'll have to wait until tonight.

My fingers skate down her chest, flicking at her nipple before squeezing it gently. I swear I hear Brittany purr. Apparently, that's all it takes to make my cock hard again. Okay, who am I kidding? It was full-on throbbing the second her naked ass jumped out of the bed, putting all of her glorious curves on display. But now…now I'm rock solid, and the object of my affection is trying to leave.

Out of nowhere, Brittany starts laughing. She pulls back just enough to look down at my straining erection. "No." Shaking her head, she places both hands on my chest and nudges me away. "I have to go. If I miss brunch, my mother will know that something is up and she won't stop until she figures out what it is."

"Something is up," I say, waggling my eyebrows. Like a predator stalking its prey, I take a measured step toward her.

"Connor," she warns, stepping back. "Don't touch me."

I stop dead in my tracks. No means *no*, and I don't take something like that lightly. I just don't like hearing it come from her mouth. "Why can't I touch you?"

"Because my body craves your body, and if you put your hands on me, I won't leave. I'll stay and let you fuck me, loving every second of it, but I really need to go."

"I love that answer, baby." Bending down, I pick up her shirt and toss it at her. "You have two seconds to put that on or I'm gonna pounce." Brittany giggles, tugging the shirt over her head. Grabbing my shorts off the floor, I slip them on and adjust my dick. "Can I touch you now?"

She nods, almost shyly, and takes a step toward me. Slipping her fingers in the waistband of my shorts, she pulls me toward her. I snake my arms around her waist. "What time do you get off?"

Her warm body is pressed against mine, but I can't seem to think about anything other than the fact that she isn't wearing pants—or underwear. All I need to do is brush my fingers along her pussy, find her clit, and she'll be mine for the next two hours.

"Connor." Fingers snap in front of my face, pulling me from my thoughts.

"Huh?"

"I asked what time you get off tonight."

"Oh, ummm"—I run a hand down my face, trying to focus on her question—"my last client is at four. I should be done by five-thirty."

"Perfect," she says, kissing my cheek. "I was thinking I could make you supper."

"What are you going to make?"

"I'm not sure yet. I'll surprise you. Is there anything you don't like?"

"Are you kidding?" I say, laughing. "Hell no. I'll eat just about anything."

Brittany smiles, giving me a soft kiss before she starts rummaging around for the rest of her clothes. I watch her get dressed, all the while wondering how strange it is that I'm already missing the feel of her body against mine.

Get a grip, Connor. She's two feet away, and you'll see her tonight.

"Okay." She smooths her hands down the front of her wrinkled shirt. "I'll see you tonight?"

"Yep. My place or yours?"

"Yours. Casey will be home, and if you come to our place, we'll never get rid of her." With one last peck on the cheek, Brittany is out of my bedroom and moving down the hall at a fast clip. Following behind her, I open the door and smack her ass as she walks out.

Twirling around, she points a finger at me. The smirk on her face tells me that she isn't actually mad. I'd bet just about anything that she secretly enjoyed it.

Chapter 13

Connor

POKING MY HEAD AROUND THE SHOWER CURTAIN, I listen carefully. I swear I just heard someone knock on my door. A few seconds pass and I hear it again. "Shit." Turning off the shower, I grab a towel and wrap it around me, knotting it at the waist. The knock becomes more insistent, and I pick up my pace in case it's Brittany and she forgot something. I skid to a halt, nearly falling flat on my ass as I yank open the front door.

My shoulders deflate when I find Logan standing in my doorway. "Hey."

"Don't sound so excited to see me," she says, pushing her way into my house. "If I didn't know better, I'd think you were hoping I was someone else."

"As a matter of fact," I say, shutting the door behind her, "I *was* hoping you were someone else."

She winces, feigning pain. "Ouch. No wonder you haven't called me back." Cocking her hip, Logan narrows her eyes. "What's her name and how long until I get my best friend back? And why in the hell am I just hearing about her now?"

"You called?" Brushing past Logan, I walk into the kitchen and grab my phone off the counter. Sure enough, I've missed three calls since last night. I should probably feel bad, but I don't. Mainly because I was too preoccupied enjoying who I was with. "Her name is Brittany. You're just now hearing about her because we've only been seeing each other for a few days, and what makes you think it won't last long?"

"Because it won't." Logan walks over and stands next to me. "It never does. You gave up fucking and started dating, but your standards are too high. No woman ever measures up."

"What's wrong with a guy wanting a smart, sexy, funny, caring woman who has dreams and goals and actually goes after them?" I ask, feeling more than a little put off by her assessment that Brittany and I won't work out. "Why shouldn't I wait for a woman with all of those qualities?"

Logan's face softens, and I remind myself she's just looking out for me. Plus, I'll just have to prove her wrong. Leaning down, I press a kiss to her cheek. "Besides, you're all of those things."

"Ooh, you're good," she says, wrapping her arms around my stomach. "So this Brittany…she's all of those things?"

Logan gives me one tight squeeze before pulling away, her question lingering in the air. I don't answer right away. Logan doesn't show affection very often, mostly because of her childhood. Being neglected for years on end will do that to a person. I'm guessing that not hearing back from me—and quite possibly the mention of Brittany—has left her feeling a little insecure. She's reaching out, needing to know I'm still here. I know this girl better than she knows herself.

"Hey," I say, snagging her arm when she turns toward my refrigerator. "I'm sorry I didn't call you back."

She shrugs, but it's half-assed and I know I need to give her more. "She consumes me," I say, breathing out the words. "When I'm with Brittany, I forget everything else around me. But that's no excuse. I should've checked my phone and called you back. Please forgive me?" I ask, jutting my lip out, mostly because I know she has a weakness for my pouty face.

I really do feel bad. Logan is the closest thing to family I have, and it devastates me to know she's hurting because of me.

"I forgive you," she mumbles, grabbing a bottle of water from the fridge. She twists the top off and takes a swig. "So I guess this means you wouldn't consider moving to Tennessee with me if I asked?"

"What?" My eyes widen, my brain processing what she just said. "Oh my gosh, Lo, you got the job?"

She nods, smiling wide. Grabbing her by the waist, I spin her around and she squeals with laughter. *I fucking love that sound.*

"Holy shit." Putting her back on her feet, I grip her shoulders. "You're leaving?" My mind races, trying to decide what this means for her...for us.

"I am." Placing the bottle of water on the table, she wrings her hands together. "But I'm nervous, you know? This is a big move."

"It is, but you've worked so hard for it. You deserve this."

"Really?" Her dark brown eyes search mine.

"Of course." Taking her hand, I lead her to the living room. She sits down on the couch and I move to sit next to her before remembering I'm wearing nothing but a towel. Holding up a finger, I motion for her to give me a second. Then I rush down the hall to my bedroom, where I make quick work of putting on some clothes. When I walk back into the living room, Logan is reclining on the couch.

"Talk to me," I say, swatting at her legs so I can sit down next to her.

Sitting up, she props her elbows on her knees and drops her head into her hands. Her dark brown hair falls around her shoulders, acting as a curtain. "I'm scared."

"Of what? You're finally getting out of this hellhole, so what on earth are you scared of?"

"This hellhole is my home." Lifting her head, she glares at me. "This is all I've known. Plus..." Her words trail off as she purses her lips.

"Plus, what?"

"*You're* my home. I don't want to live where you aren't, Connor."

"Logan." Sighing, I scoot next to her. She slips her tiny hand in mine and I squeeze it lightly. "It doesn't matter how far away you live, you will always be a huge part of my life. I will always be here for you."

"So if I beg you to come with me, would you consider it?" she asks without an ounce of humor.

"Wow." Pulling my hand from hers, I run my fingers through my hair. "Logan."

"Don't." Shaking her head, she pushes up from the

couch. "I shouldn't have asked that."

"That's not it," I say, trying to figure out the best way to say this. "You know I would love to go with you. The thought of not seeing you and talking to you all the time terrifies me. But I've got InkSlingers now, and I'm not ready to leave that behind."

She nods, swallowing hard. "And Brittany. I guess you have her now, too?"

"Please don't. This has nothing to do with Brittany. Yes, I really like her. Yes, she's everything I've been looking for in a woman. But we've only been seeing each other for a *few days*. I'm staying because this is my home, and I don't *want* to leave. I want to keep building up the shop and see where it goes." I blowing out a harsh breath. "And yes, I'm anxious to see where this thing with Brittany goes too, but I want to stay here because I'm finally happy. And you know I've worked really hard to find my happy."

"Ugh," she grunts, tossing her head back. "I know. I know you're happy. But the selfish part of me wants you to be happy where *I* am." She takes a deep breath. "Connor"—Logan looks up at me, a wave of uncertainty swirling through her eyes—"I've never been on my own. Not really. You've always been a hop, skip, and a jump away, ready and willing to pick up whatever mess I've made. What if I can't do this on my own?

What if I fail miserably?"

"Don't—"

"And what if I lose you?" she asks, cutting me off. "What if you forget all about me? You're the only family I have, and I don't want to lose you." Her voice cracks on the last word, slicing my heart in two.

"Stop it." Hooking an arm around her neck, I hug her tight. "You *are* my family. Nothing is going to change that. I don't care that we don't share the same blood. You are my sister in every sense of the word. You've seen me through so much bullshit, and I could never forget that. I could never forget *you*."

"I'm sorry." She sniffs, swiping at her face when a tear runs down her cheek. "I know I'm being an emotional female about this. It's all just happening so fast."

"Is it?" I ask, pulling back to look her in the eyes. "You've been going to school, planning for this moment, and when you filled out the application, you knew it was in a different state." Logan worked two jobs to put herself through nursing school. She knew immediately that she wanted to work in a trauma ICU. Apparently, it's difficult to get that particular position right out of school. So when she found out about a hospital that was accepting applications for a one-year paid internship at their trauma ICU with the option to stay on full-time afterward, she jumped on it.

"I hate it when you're right," she mumbles, burying her face in my chest.

"You know," I say, deciding now is not the time to gloat about always being right, "more than likely you're going to get out there and make a whole new set of friends. Before I know it, you'll be bringing home a boyfriend for me to meet. And I'm warning you now, as your brother and best friend, I *will* intimidate the hell outta him."

Logan laughs, and it's as though I can feel some of the weight being lifted from her shoulders. "You think?"

"I don't think...I know. You're intelligent, beautiful, and you have this incredible heart. Any man would be more than lucky to have you in his life. Myself included."

Taking a deep breath, Logan blows it out slowly. "Okay, I'm going to do this. I'm moving to Tennessee." Her smile grows. Pulling out of my arms, she rubs her hands together. "Holy crap. I'm moving to Tennessee. I'm going to be a full-time nurse." Her eyes widen, almost comically, and I'm getting the feeling she's moments away from either laughing hysterically or crying. At this point, it could go either way.

"I'm so proud of you, Lo."

Her eyes glisten. "Thank you. We've come a long

way, haven't we?"

"I couldn't have done it without you."

"I guess we got lucky getting sent to that last foster home, huh?"

"Damn straight. If it wasn't for that godforsaken place, I wouldn't have you in my life."

"And we wouldn't have met Carter." Logan looks down for a beat before glancing back up. "I miss him," she whispers. "Do you think he'd be proud of me?"

"I miss him, too. And he'd be *so* proud of you."

"Thank you." Logan wipes her hands over her face and straightens her shoulders as though she's pulling herself together. "Speaking of Carter," she says, "you probably have to be at work soon, don't you? Hell, I have to be at work and here I am blubbering all over the place."

"Actually," I say, glancing at the clock on the wall, "I probably should finish getting ready so I can head in. I already took a shower, but I still need to trim my beard."

"Oh!" Logan waves her hands in the air as though she just remembered something really important. "*That's* why I was trying to call you. My water heater went out. Do you mind if I swing by tonight after work and get cleaned up?"

"Damn it," I say, groaning. "Why didn't you tell

me? You know that shit pisses me off. I would've gone over to take a look at it for you."

Logan cocks an eyebrow, giving me her classic don't-get-sassy-with-me look. "Ummm...*you're* the one who didn't answer your phone. And there isn't anything you could've done anyway," she says, waving me off. "I have to have a new water heater put in, but my landlord says they can't come until tomorrow."

"Still pisses me off," I grumble. "But since you're going to be here, why don't you plan on staying for supper? Brittany is cooking."

"Will she mind?" Logan asks, walking toward the pantry. "Can I steal a Pop-Tart? I was in such a hurry this morning I forgot breakfast."

"I don't think she'll mind, but I'll talk to her and make sure. And eat the chocolate ones; that strawberry one is mine."

She nods and reaches for the Pop-Tarts on the top shelf, but she's not quite tall enough. I take a step toward her but stop when she grabs a chair from the table. My mind drifts to Logan's water heater. Who is she going to call when she's in Tennessee and has a problem? Who's going to fix her garbage disposal or change the batteries in her smoke detector?

I watch silently as she slides the chair toward the shelves, steps up, grabs the box, and puts the chair back. It was a simple task—and obviously not all problems will be fixed quite so easily—but it reminds me that she's a big girl and fully capable of solving her own issues. And I'll still be here for the ones she can't.

"Why are you staring at me like that?"

"You're going to do great in Tennessee," I say sincerely. Logan tilts her head, probably wondering why in the world I went from Pop-Tarts back to Tennessee.

I'm two steps down the hall when she calls my name. "Connor?"

"Yeah?" I peek over my shoulder to find her standing in the hallway. "Thank you…for everything. I can't wait to meet Brittany tonight."

I smile. "You're going to love her."

"I already figured as much." She smiles back, a look of pride and—most importantly—acceptance shining from her face.

Everything is going to be okay.

For the both of us.

Chapter 14

Brittany

*T*HIS IS CRAZY, I THINK TO MYSELF, STARING AT THE door. Is it proper dating etiquette to drop in on someone at work just to say 'hey'? Probably not, but Connor does own the place and I'm in the area, so what the hell. I tug the door open and the familiar bell dings, signaling my entry.

Everyone in the shop turns toward me. I freeze, surprised at the amount of people in here. Honestly, I thought it would just be Connor and a client. Nope, there's actually…one, two, three, four—

"Can I help you?"

I turn toward the front desk and the tiny girl seat-ed behind it. "Um, I'm here to see Connor."

"Good timing," she says. "He just finished with a client. He's in the pisser."

Okay. That's not at all what I expected her to say, but she's cute in a gothic Tinker Bell sort of way so I decide to go with it. "Is it okay if I wait?"

Tinker Bell shrugs, popping the gum in her mouth. "Suit yourself. You can keep me company. I'm hella bored."

I stick my hand out. "I'm Brittany."

She looks at my outstretched hand hesitantly before slipping her much smaller, more delicate one into mine. "Nora."

"It's a pleasure to meet you."

"Are you sure you're in the right place?" she asks, scrunching her nose.

"Hell yes, she's in the right place." Turning around, I come face-to-face with Connor. "I see you've met Nora," he says, snaking an arm around my waist. I step into him, the front of our bodies molding together.

"I did meet her." My words come out way too husky for my liking, so I clear my voice. "She's very sweet. You're very sweet," I say, looking over Connor's shoulder. Nora is staring at us, mouth agape. I look around, and everyone else in the shop is staring at us too. "Do I have toilet paper hanging out of the back of my pants?" I whisper, pressing in closer to Connor. He smiles, slow and sexy. "No," he whispers. "You're just that fucking gorgeous, and they're all wondering why in the hell you're here to see me."

"Psssh." Slapping at Connor's chest, I push away. "I highly doubt that."

Connor rolls his eyes. "Whatever." Gripping my hand firmly in his, Connor pulls me to his station. "So, to what do I owe this wonderful surprise visit?"

Once we're out of sight, Connor drops to a chair and tugs me onto his lap. Large, warm hands find their way up the back of my shirt, and for the life of me I can't remember what he just asked me. "What?" He continues trailing his fingertips across my skin and my eyes nearly roll back in my head.

"I asked what brought you by," he says, nuzzling the side of my neck.

"Oh, yeah…I was in the area. I need to go by the Chef's Nook down the street, so I figured I'd drop by."

Connor's deft fingers travel around my waist, stroking my stomach, and a shiver races up my spine. "What do you need from that place?" he asks, seemingly oblivious to the way he's torturing me.

My body is thrumming with sexual energy, and if I don't get out of here soon, I'm going to beg him to fuck me right here in this chair. "You have to stop touching me," I demand, earning myself a bright, white smile from Connor.

"Sorry, I can't do that. Now tell me what you're getting at the Chef's Nook."

"A pan for lasagna."

Connor's hands stop. "You're making me lasagna?"

"Is that okay?" I ask, suddenly unsure of my supper choice. He did tell me that was his favorite food, right? Shit. Maybe I was so damn horny I didn't hear him correctly.

"It's perfect."

"Good. I realized when I got home that I don't have the right-sized pan. It might still be in storage, but there's no way in hell I'm digging through that mess so I'll just buy a new one."

"Don't." Connor shakes his head. "I've got every size pan you can imagine in my kitchen. Just go borrow what you need. Hell, make dinner at my place if you want. In fact," he says, waggling his eyebrows, "I wouldn't complain one bit if I came home and you were wearing nothing but an apron. That would actually be really fucking awesome."

"Is sex all you think about?" I ask with mock annoyance.

"No," he says, pressing his lips to the base of my

neck. The scruff on his jaw abrades my skin, and I squeeze my thighs together in a desperate attempt to control my ever-growing need. "All I think about is you."

My body shudders at his words. Damn he's good. "I like that," I say, cupping his face in my hands. "Because I can't stop thinking about you either."

A deep growl rumbles from Connor's chest. "You can't say those things to me when I'm at work because it makes me want to lay you flat on that table," he says, motioning toward the tiny table with supplies scattered on the surface. "And I *cannot* lay you flat on that table." He pauses and glances at said tiny table. "Well, I could, but we'd end up flat on our asses."

I push up from Connor's lap. "Tonight you can lay me on any surface you want. How about that?" I whisper, giving him a quick peck on the lips.

"Fuuuuuck," he says, reaching for my arm.

Laughing, I sidestep his grabby hand. He attempts to glare at me, but it lacks the necessary edge and I end up laughing harder. "Later, I promise. Now are you sure you don't mind if I borrow a pan?"

"Fine." He sighs, reminding me of a petulant child. Normally, I would find that annoying, but when Connor does it, I find it cute. "And you're more than welcome to borrow it." Connor stands up and leads me out of his workstation toward the front door. "You can go in through the garage. My code is 9080."

"Thank you."

"You're making me lasagna. Trust me, I should be the one thanking you. Oh! By the way"—he snaps his fingers—"is it okay if Logan joins us for dinner tonight?"

"Absolutely. I'd love to meet your best friend." Lifting up on my tiptoes, I brush my mouth against Connor's ear. "Just make sure Logan is gone by dessert. I've got a can of whipped cream I was planning to bring over."

"Leave. Now." I bust up laughing when Connor all but shoves me out the front door. He immediately yanks me back in and gives me a searing kiss that earns us several catcalls from the guys in the shop, and then he shoves me back out again. "Now go."

"Goodbye, Connor." I walk out of InkSlingers, and my body feels as though I'm floating down the sidewalk. My heart is full, my soul is happy, and I'm afraid this goofy-ass smile will be permanently etched on my face.

Holy shit, I'm in love.

Chapter 15

Brittany

"THIS SMELLS FANTASTIC." KEEPING HIS HANDS on the hot rags, Connor takes the steaming dish from my hands.

"I slaved all day over a hot stove for you," I say jokingly as I follow him into the kitchen. "So now what are you going to do for me?"

Connor puts the lasagna on the stove top. "Where's the whipped cream?" he whispers, wrapping his arms around my waist.

Bringing my hands to his chest, I slide them up his neck. Then I cup his face in my hands and kiss him softly. "It's already in your fridge," I mumble, my lips brushing his. "I brought it over when I borrowed the casserole dish. Wasn't sure what Logan would think if I walked in with a can of whipped cream and no dessert to go with it."

"But you did bring dessert." Connor's husky voice wraps around my body. "I plan to lick it off of you here"—he trails his lips to the base of my neck—"and here"—his tongue darts out, making a path along the tops of my breasts—"and we can't forget about here," he says, slipping his hand between my legs.

I'm ready to rip my clothes off so he can fuck me right here in the kitchen, company be damned.

How in the hell does he do that?

"Connor." I hate to admit it, but yes, I just whimpered his name.

He hoists me up on the counter and pushes my legs apart, making room for his big, sexy body.

"When you say my name like that, it makes me want to do dirty, *dirty* things to you." His mouth descends and he attacks my neck. My head drops back between my shoulders, giving him better access. There is no way we're going to make it through—

"Connor, can I get another towel?" My head snaps forward at the sound of a delicate voice—a delicate *female* voice. Then, as a half-naked woman rounds the corner, my heart seizes in my chest. Long, dark hair spills over her shoulders, water dripping down her bare arms, and miles upon miles of long legs are on display.

I think I'm going to throw up.

"Oh, shit." The woman's steps falter when she locks eyes with me. "I'm so sorry," she says, fisting her hand in the knotted towel, just above her breasts. She looks as shocked as I probably do.

Connor groans, dropping his head to my shoulder before turning around. "Logan, this is—*holy shit, woman!* Go put some clothes on."

Logan.

Connor's best friend is named Logan.

Oh no. *No-no-no-no.*

"I need another towel," she says, right before giving me a bashful smile. "I really am sorry." She takes a step toward us and my entire body freezes. "I don't usually"—her words trail off and she waves her hand in the air—"you know, walk around here...like this."

I'm at a complete loss for words as she stares at me, presumably waiting for me to tell her that's it's all right and I understand. But it's not all right, and I most certainly do *not* understand. And—oh great—now Connor is staring at me.

"You know what?" Logan says, gesturing toward the hall. "I don't need that other towel. I'll just...go."

She scurries off and I watch her until she disappears. I can see out of the corner of my eye that Connor hasn't taken his eyes off me.

"Hey." Connor puts his face in front of mine. "Are you okay?" He runs soothing hands down each of my arms, and my body stiffens. Scooting forward, I nudge him back, and when there's enough room, I slide off the counter.

"So…" Running my shaky hands down the front of my shirt, I sidestep Connor. "That's your best friend Logan?" I'm proud that I was able to keep my voice from wavering because, really, I don't want Logan to be his best friend.

"It is." Those two little words are said with so much caution that I know he knows I have a problem with it. "Are you okay?"

I would be, except you forgot to mention that Logan is of the vagina-yielding species.

My lungs fight to suck in air, but it's getting more difficult with each passing second. Pressure builds behind my eyes and I blink several times to keep the tears at bay, though I know it's only a matter of time. "Wow." I blow out a long breath. "Your best friend is a woman."

"Brittany." Connor steps in front of me. Tilting his head to the side, he studies me. We're not touching, but God do I want to touch him. *So bad.* I want him to wrap me in his arms, tell me this is all some horrible mix-up, and promise me that everything will be okay. But that won't happen and I need to quit being so damn naïve. "I'm sorry I didn't tell you that Logan was a girl. To be honest, I didn't even think about it. She's like a sister to me."

Funny, Tyson said the exact same thing.

How in the hell did I not see this coming? "Of course she is," I mumble. My heart is screaming at me not to make any rash decisions, but my heart is also the traitorous bastard that got me here in the first place.

I look at the front door and then down the hall. Logan hasn't reemerged and I'm wondering if she has her ear pressed to a door, trying to listen. Bile rises in my throat and I swallow hard. I'm seconds away from losing my shit, and I sure as hell won't lose it with another woman here. "I need to go," I say, scurrying toward the front door.

"Wait." Connor snags my wrist and spins me around. Brows dipped low, he shakes his head. "Are you upset because I didn't tell you Logan is a girl?" he asks. "Because I would've told you if I thought it was going to be an issue—hell, if I'd even thought about it." His voice is no longer gentle and careful, instead it sounds as though he's frustrated.

Welcome to the club, buddy.

"I'm sure you would have."

"What's that supposed to mean?" Releasing my wrist, Connor steps back and runs a hand through his hair. Lacing his fingers behind his neck, he releases a heavy sigh. "I'm so fucking lost right now."

"She's your best friend," I state simply, as though he should understand. I know in my heart that he doesn't, but we've already established what an idiot my heart is.

"So what?"

So what? *So what?* I'll show him *so what!*

"You have a key to her place." I wasn't asking, I was making a statement, but Connor answers me anyway.

"Yes, I do."

"How often do you use it?" I don't even know why I'm asking. I guess I'm hoping that if he only uses it once a month then maybe, just maybe, I could find a way to move past this.

"What the fuck?" he growls, tossing his hands up at his side. "I don't know. A couple of times a week, maybe. But what the hell does that have to do with anything?"

"Have you slept with her?"

His jaw drops open, but he quickly recovers. "No,"

he snaps. "I haven't *fucked* her if that's what you're asking. Look, I made a mistake. I should've told you and I'm sorry. Please"—he shakes his head—"don't do this. I know what you're doing, and I'm asking you not to do this."

"You don't know what I'm doing," I say with a tad more bite than I intended. Connor's eyes widen. It looks like we're having our first official fight…and ironically, our last. "Do you love her?" I want to punch myself in the fucking face for asking. It's completely unfair to him—and to Logan—but I need to hear him say it.

It doesn't matter what his answer is, I tell myself. *You need to leave now. Make a clean break while you can.*

"Of course I love her. She's my best friend."

My heart twists painfully inside my chest. It's as if I'm right back where I was when Tyson left. I can't do that again. I can't pour my heart and soul into someone—and I would've poured my heart and soul into Connor—and risk being left again. I've regained some strength over the years, but I'm not that strong.

"I'm sorry," I say, all of the fight draining out of me. I won't resort to acting like a jealous teenager. Twisting my hands in front of me, I will myself to find the courage to walk away. After a deep breath, I say,

"I'm sorry for leading you on like this. I know I'm not making any sense, but…but I can't do this with you."

The air grows thick with tension. Connor purses his lips but doesn't say a word. Instead, he walks straight to the door. Twisting the knob, he pulls it open and steps back, giving me plenty of room to pass. I walk toward him, hating the way his gaze drops to the floor. The tic in his jaw catches my attention.

Connor doesn't understand what's going on and that doesn't sit well with me. If I'm going to walk out of here, never to return, then he at least deserves to know why.

"I was engaged," I blurt out. Connor looks up and now it's my turn to look down. I don't want to see the pity I know he'll offer, because that's what everyone does.

Clearing my throat, I start talking, and I don't stop until I've told him everything. "We were college sweethearts, together for years. In 2006, we applied to med school in New York and we both got in." I smile to myself, remembering how happy I was. The same kind of happy I was just minutes ago. "Right before the big move, Tyson's best friend—*who happened to be a woman*—confessed her love for him." I suck in a shuddery breath. I've worked so hard to forget that horrible night, and reliving isn't going to be fun.

"She begged him to stay and give her a chance, but he didn't. He walked away from her—he chose me. I was thrilled because, in the back of my mind, I'd always thought he had a thing for her, but I had to have been wrong, right?" I shrug. "That was his opportunity to be with her and he didn't take it. Anyway," I say, rubbing a hand over my face, "we moved to New York and started our lives there. The years went by, and like any normal couple, our relationship progressed. One year over Christmas break, Tyson brought me back home, and after asking my parents for permission, he proposed."

Squeezing my eyes shut, I allow the warmth and love from that moment to seep back into my heart, a glimpse of what true love—or what I thought was true love—felt like. "You know that old saying that hindsight is twenty-twenty? Well, it's true."

Connor has been eerily silent and I peek up at him. I'm shocked when I don't see pity swimming in his eyes. Empathy, yes, but no pity, and in this moment my respect for him grows. "We weren't living our lives. I was living *my* life and Tyson was living around me. We were merely existing, and I wish I would've noticed it sooner. But it was too late. I came home from the hospital one night and found him sitting in the living room surrounded by suitcases."

The pain from that moment pierces my heart. Lifting my hand, I prepare to rub away the ache—the same ache I get in the left side of my chest any time I think about that night. Only this time, the ache doesn't come.

"Tell me the rest." Connor's voice is raspy, his eyes filled with emotion.

"He left me. Broke off the engagement, moved back home, and eventually won back the girl he truly was in love with."

"His best friend." It isn't a question. Connor's a smart man and he easily puts two and two together.

I nod. "Her name is Harley and, believe it or not," I say, laughing mirthlessly, "I actually like her. I don't want to like her, but I do. And I'm sure I would like Logan as well, but I just… I can't put myself in that position again." Reaching out, I wrap my hand around the doorknob, ready to make my escape—but not before finishing the story. I've come this far, so I may as well tell him the rest. "Tyson is adopting Harley's son and they have a baby on the way. Three weeks ago they tied the knot."

Connor's eyes widen. "*Ad astra per aspera*," he murmurs.

I scrunch my nose. "Huh?"

"Your tattoo." Connor takes a hesitant step toward

me. "You came into my shop on their wedding day. That's why you got the tattoo."

I take a deep breath but it catches in my throat, and I close my eyes to try and stop the building tears. There's no point in denying it, but I also don't want to talk about it. Opening my eyes, I step through the doorway and spin around to get one last look at Connor. His anger and frustration from moments ago are completely gone and his eyes are pleading with me to stay.

But I just can't. By staying, I'm opening myself up to the kind of pain I experienced before, and that's exactly what I've been afraid of.

I had a momentary lapse in judgment when I decided to let Connor in. My mistake. Either way, I'll move on, and so will he.

Fuck. I don't like the sound of that at all, but it's for the best.

"The tattoo you got that day, what does it mean?" he asks, almost frantically.

"A rough road leads to the stars." I don't wait around to see his reaction or give him time to respond. "Goodbye, Connor." I shut the door before he has the chance to stop me from leaving. Pressing my back against the wood, I squeeze my eyes shut and blow out a long, slow breath.

A few moments ago when I was talking about Tyson, I'd waited for my chest to ache. It never did. But now that I've walked away from Connor, the pain is back. This time, however, it's so much more than an ache—it's a stabbing pain that not only slices through my heart, it pierces my soul.

Chapter 16

Brittany

IT'S BEEN THREE DAYS SINCE I'VE SEEN CONNOR. Four thousand three hundred and twenty seconds, to be exact, and every single one of those I've been thinking about him. Since that night, he's left me seven voicemails and fifteen texts, begging me to talk to him, and he's stopped by the house twice. I know I'm a coward, but I just couldn't. One look in that man's eyes and I would've caved.

I keep telling myself it isn't a big deal that his best friend is a woman. Except it *is* a big deal. Being second best in someone's life isn't something I'm willing to do—not again, at least.

"Are you going to turn the TV on, or just stare at the blank screen all night?" Casey asks, walking into the living room. She falls onto the couch next to me and nudges me with her elbow.

"I kind of like the blank screen."

"Sure ya do." She glances down at her watch, a knowing look on her face when her eyes meet mine. "It's almost four."

Crossing my arms over my chest, I do my best to appear unaffected. "So?"

"Sooooo," she says. "Connor stopped by yesterday at four, and the day before that at four. I bet today won't be any different."

"Yes, well, we're over. He needs to move on. It's not like we were together long." I laugh out loud at myself for saying that. I felt more with him in those few short days than I did after years with Tyson. That should mean something, and if I wasn't being so stubborn, it probably would.

"You need to talk to him." Leave it to my little sister to try and put me in my place. "Have you at least returned any of his texts or phone calls?" I shake my head and she rolls her eyes. "You're being a little bitch."

I rear back as though she just slapped me across the face. "Whose side are you on?"

"Yours," she says. "Always yours. But even if I'm

on your side, it doesn't mean I think you're making the right decision."

"He had a half-naked woman in his house," I yell, hoping it finally sinks into her brain. "A half-naked woman who just so happens to be his best friend. Does this not sound familiar to you? Do you remember the hell Tyson put me through?"

"Of course I do," she says, understanding flashing in her eyes. "But Connor isn't Tyson."

"Tell that to my brain."

"See, that's the problem. You need to quit thinking about this with your head and start thinking about it with this big, fat muscle right here," she says, poking me in the chest. "You are a doctor, right? You know which muscle I'm talking about."

"Yes," I say, slapping her hand away. "I know which muscle you're talking about. But Case...I'm not sure I could survive another broken heart."

"Well"—she pushes up from the couch, then puts her hands on her hips—"the mopey-ass look on your face tells me you're already surviving one."

"My heart isn't breaking," I say, giving her a tremulous smile. My eyes well with tears and a few slip past my lashes. Because even as I say it, I know it isn't true. Connor and I may not have been together for very long, but I *really* did see a future together. "I wasn't in love with Connor."

"You don't have to be in love for your heart to break." Casey brushes a tear from my face and then walks away.

I'm not sure how long I sit and stare off into space, but I'm startled when a loud knock sounds at the door.

Come on, Connor. You're only making this harder on both of us.

Several seconds pass, and right when I think he gave up, another knock sounds. Maybe it's best to just get this over with now, although I feel like I've said all I needed to say. Pushing up from the couch, I open the door and come face-to-face with... "Logan."

"Hey." She waves awkwardly. "Can I come in for a second?"

"Sure." Stepping aside, I open the door wide. She walks in and follows me to the living room. Her eyes drift around my duplex. My gaze follows hers, and I realize that she must think it's odd that the place is completely bare.

"I just moved in." Scratching the top of my head, I try to come up with something to say, *something* to fill this awkward silence. I've got nothing.

"I know." Logan brings her gaze back to me. "Connor told me."

My skin prickles at the mention of his name.

"Right. Connor." Sucking my bottom lip in between my teeth, I nod.

"Connor's crazy about you."

Hold up. What did she say? I expected her to come over here and yell at me, maybe try and start some sort of catfight, but I didn't expect her to say *that*. Something on my face must clue her in to my confusion because she chuckles.

"It's true." I stare at her, trying to figure out how to respond. "Mind if I sit?" she asks.

"Please, have a seat."

She sits on the couch, scooting toward the edge, but I stay standing. Logan's shoulders droop. Her eyes fall to something in front of her, and for a brief second it's as though she's reliving some sort of memory. When she looks back up, her eyes are full of understanding. "I heard what you said to Logan. Eavesdropping isn't typically my thing, but what can I say?" she says, shrugging. "I'm a woman."

A bubble of laughter crawls up my throat and she visibly relaxes at the sound. "It's okay. I have a sister. A nosy-ass sister. I understand."

"I'm sorry that happened to you," she says, once again catching me off guard. "I can't imagine how difficult that must've been. I won't pretend to understand what it felt like, because I've never been in love. But

I do know what it's like to come second to someone else."

She's offering me an olive branch. I'm not one to look a gift horse in the mouth, so I take it. "You do?"

"Unfortunately." Logan wraps a strand of hair around her fingers, twirling it. "My dad chose his girlfriend over me. It's not something I like to think about, but I want you to know that I understand and I wouldn't wish it upon anyone," she says, looking up at me. "Did Connor tell you how we met?" she asks.

"Foster care."

"Yup. My dad neglected me and I was eventually taken away from him. I bounced around several horrible foster homes, but the day of my last move was the luckiest day of my life."

"It was?" I ask, curious. Why on earth would moving into a new foster home be the best day of someone's life?

"It was. Because that's the day I met my brother." I didn't miss that Logan emphasized the word *brother*. "Connor and I might not share the same blood, but he is my family in every sense of the word. Do I love Connor? Yes, but not the way you're afraid of. And trust me, I understand why you'd be afraid."

"You do?"

"Yes. I don't necessarily agree with it—which is

why I'm here—but I understand. Putting yourself out there like that, in the same situation you were in before? That would be terrifying. I'm not sure I could do it, so I wouldn't expect you to."

"But you just said you don't agree with me," I say, my brows dipping low.

"Yeah, well, that's the other thing I wanted to tell you. Coming in second sucks. I don't want to go through something like that again, just like you don't want to. But I'd gladly come in second *to you*."

"What?" I drop down onto the couch.

"I love Connor," she states firmly. "Nothing and no one is ever going to change that—not even you. But I'm not *in love* with him. Never have been, never will be. And the thing is, I realize Connor isn't my dad. He may put you first, which he should, but he wouldn't forget about me. He won't treat me the way my dad did. And he wouldn't treat you the way Tyson did."

My lips press together in a frown. "I don't know, Logan." Bringing my hand to my mouth, I pull at my lip, my mind digesting everything she just said.

"Do you want to know why I'd gladly take second place to you?" she asks hopefully. I nod. "Because you make him happy. You're so different than any girl he's been with, and trust me, I've been there for all of them. He smiles every time he says your name, even after you left him."

My eyes burn, tears pushing against the confines of my lashes. Logan didn't have to come over here and tell me all of this, but she did because she wants her best friend to be happy. And apparently, she realizes the person who makes him happy is me. The old Brit would've likely found a way to discredit everything she's saying, but the new Brit wants desperately to believe it. Because the new Brit can't say Connor's name without smiling, too.

A small grin tugs at the corner of my mouth. Maybe my heart was right to take a chance on Connor. Maybe it learned its lesson the first time and recognizes Connor for who he is—the type of man to love me the way I deserve to be loved.

"I hope that smile means something good," Logan says, her eyes bright with hope.

Regret quickly overshadows my moment of happiness as I recall the way I so easily dismissed Connor. What if doesn't forgive me? What if he thinks I'm batshit crazy? What if I threw away my one chance at real happiness?

"No," Logan snaps, catching my attention. "Your smile is fading. Why in the world is your smile fading?"

"What if I already ruined everything? It wasn't

like we were together long. What if he's decided I'm a flight risk?"

"Girl..." Logan clucks her tongue. She stands up and I follow suit. "We're all flight risks. It's what makes us human. And guess what?"

"What?"

"Humans make mistakes, and the really awesome humans—like Connor—forgive those mistakes."

"Did he tell you he'd forgive me?"

"Hell no," she scoffs. "And trust me, I've tried to talk to him about it, but all I've gotten are grunts and nods. You know, the typical male bullshit. That's the other reason I knew you were in his life for good." I cock a brow, urging her to continue, and she rolls her eyes. "Connor tells me everything about everything... except when it comes to you."

Wow. That's surprising, especially if they're best friends. Tyson used to tell Harley *everything*. It was one of the things that pissed me off the most. Maybe appearances aren't the only way that Connor and Tyson are different.

"I've spent the last three days begging him to give me the nitty-gritty details, but the brute won't budge. His lips are sealed because you're important to him. And if you're important to him, you're important to me."

Logan barely gets the last word out before I yank her into my arms. At first she doesn't hug me back, but that's okay; I don't take offense to it. I just keep squeezing until she finally does. It starts with a pat on my back and then her grip on me tightens.

"Maybe we can both come first," I say, wanting so badly to be Logan's friend.

"Nah," she says. "You should come first. That's how it should be. Plus, I'm moving to Tennessee."

Gripping her shoulders, I pull back until we're eye to eye. "You're moving to Tennessee?"

"Yep. Connor didn't tell you?"

I shake my head. "But I didn't exactly give him the chance."

"Well, I am, and I need someone here to look after my brother. I need to know he's taken care of. And I could *really* use someone that's willing to help me out when I bring a cowboy back home with me."

Furrowing my brows, I try to picture Connor meeting Logan's cowboy boyfriend. Connor in his Chucks, long hair, beard, and colorful tattoos, versus a Stetson-wearing cowboy. That could be really interesting. "I promise to run interference," I say.

"See?" she says, nudging my shoulder. "This is going to work out perfectly." Logan's eyes soften. "Who knows, maybe I'll get a sister out of it." She tried to sound flippant, but I could see past her façade.

"I think that sounds fantastic."

Logan's face lights up, and for several seconds we both just stare at each other.

"Well, I better get going," she says, nodding toward the door.

"Are you going to Connor's?" I ask.

"No," she says, winking at me. "You are."

Chapter 17

Connor

I**T'S BEEN THREE DAYS SINCE** B**RITTANY WALKED OUT** of my house. I shouldn't care, considering I'd only known her for a hot second, but boy was it a hot second. The best damn hot second of my life.

And that right there is exactly why I can't let her go.

I can't…and won't.

She stunned the hell outta me with the story about her fiancé. As much as I hated to hear what happened to her, it explains her reaction to Logan being a female. I can't say I blame her for being upset. If the roles were reversed, I probably would've lost my shit, too.

My heart broke for her, and by the time I came up with something to say, she was already gone. I pounded on her front door for nearly an hour, begging her to talk to me. It wasn't until Logan grabbed my arm and physically pulled me back to my house that I finally gave up. But even then I didn't really give up, because I can't stop thinking about her and I'd be lying if I said I haven't been plotting ways to get her back.

I've been with my fair share of women, but not one has affected me the way Brittany has. Her big blue eyes peeking up at me under thick, dark lashes made my heart flip over in my chest. The dimples in her cheeks, winking at me every time she laughed, caused me to lose my breath. But what affected me the most was feeling her body shudder under the touch of my hand. *That* feeling made me want to stand on a mountain and pound my chest, claiming her as mine.

So right now I'm doing the only thing I can do. I'm holding on to those moments while I give her time. Unfortunately for her, the more time I spend thinking, the more pissed off I get.

What Tyson did was shitty, but I'm not Tyson.

Clenching my jaw, I stand up. What the hell am I supposed to do? How do I handle this? A part of me thinks I need to sit back and just give her time to miss me; that she'll realize what a terrible mistake she made.

The other part of me wants to tear into her for screwing with my feelings the way she has. I let her into my life, I bent my rules, and this is the shit she pulls?

Fuck.

She's got me so fucking tied up in knots it isn't even funny. It's infuriating, actually.

My frustration is at an all-time high. I pace the living room several times before deciding that giving her space is the wrong choice. I'm not sure giving her a piece of my mind is the right way to go, but it's what I'm going to do, and damn it, she's going to listen.

Leaving the house, I stomp toward Brittany's side of the duplex. Before I make it to her porch, the front door flies open, revealing what appears to be a deliriously happy Brittany and a smiling Logan.

What. The. Hell.

Brittany's gaze lands on me. Her smile falters just a fraction, the happiness seemingly replaced with uncertainty. *There's no room for uncertainty now, sweetheart.* You said your piece, and now it's time I said mine.

She takes a step toward me. Straightening my back, I square my shoulders and stalk toward her. Something in my approach must confuse her because she stops and flicks her eyes to Logan before bringing them back to me.

"Goodbye, Logan," I say without sparing her a glance. Logan snickers, but out of the corner of my eye I see her scurry toward her car. I walk straight over to Brittany, not stopping until we're toe to toe. The air around us crackles. It's something I'd gotten used to, something I'm going to miss if I can't get her to see she's making a huge fucking mistake. Something I'm afraid I'll never feel again with anyone else.

Chin held high, I glare at Brittany. Gorgeous blue eyes are watching me carefully, sparkling with what looks a whole hell of a lot like hope. Her hair is pulled up in a bun on top of her head, loose strands floating around her face, and her shirt is a rumpled mess. She looks so different like this; not at all like the put-together doctor she is. I like this side of her. I like every side of her.

I've never wanted so badly to both kiss a woman and physically shake her as I do in this moment.

"I'm so fucking pissed at you right now," I say, grinding the words out. Brittany scrunches her nose at the tone of my voice. She's so damn adorable when she does that. My body deflates, my frustration waning.

Oh hell no, Connor, I think to myself, *you will not get distracted. You came here because you have something to say, and—damn it—you're going to say it.*

"We need to talk, and by that I mean I'm going to

157

do the talking and you're going to listen."

Brittany's brows are now nearly touching her hairline. She plants a fist on her hip. "Well, I have a few things to say, too," she says with just as much bite.

"You've already talked and now it's my turn." My eyes lock on her plump lower lip as she sucks it into her mouth. Even though it's only been a few days, I already recognize this as a nervous habit.

Pulling my eyes to hers, I swear I see a hint of amusement flash across her face. "Cut the bullshit," I snap, watching her face fall. "This isn't funny. You're blaming me for the mistakes of that prick who broke your heart." Nothing like throwing it all out there, and there's no stopping now. "I'm nothing like him. I would never hurt you because I care about you, and hurting you would hurt me. But you don't feel the same way, do you?" I ask, not really looking for an answer.

"That's not—"

"Because if you felt the same way," I say, interrupting her, "then you wouldn't have walked away so easily. Did you even try giving us a chance, or were you so scared of getting hurt again that you looked for an out any place you could find it?" She opens her mouth, but I'm not done. "And I handed it to you on a silver fucking platter, didn't I? I gave you the one reason to bail that everyone would understand."

"Connor—"

"This is pointless," I say, gripping the back of my neck. "You've already put me in the same category as him. There's no sense trying to defend myself. But you know what? I shouldn't have to defend myself, because I deserve better than that. I'm a good guy who would give every single part of myself, and I deserve that in return." Brittany's eyes glisten under the dull light of the falling sun. Her tears rip through my heart, the sharp pain radiating to my soul. I can tell my words hit their mark.

I hurt her.

I just said I would never hurt her, yet I did it anyway.

I'm no better than she is. Maybe we're better off not together after all.

Taking a deep breath, I find my resolve. "I can't do this." I glance at my house. Maybe it's time to make my exit.

"Are you done spewing all of that bullshit?"

My head snaps back, her words a slap in the face. "You've got to be kidding me."

"I came out here to tell you I'm sorry," she says, the expression on her face much softer than her voice.

"You did?"

"Yes, but—"

"No buts." Grabbing her chin, I demand her attention. "Tell me," I plead. The energy that was coursing through my body is quickly transforming from frustration to hope.

"I'm sorry—"

My arms wrap around her before she even finishes apologizing. Pulling her body flush against mine, I hold her close…and this time I'm not letting her go. Relief washes through me, because being without her was going to hurt like a bitch.

Brittany laughs, her face squished against my chest. "You don't even know what I was going to say," she mumbles against my shirt.

Chills race down my spine, unease settling in my gut. Pulling back, I narrow my eyes.

"No," Brittany says quickly. "I didn't mean it like that. I do apologize, but I want to *finish* apologizing."

Lips parting, I sigh in relief. "Does your apology end with us being together?"

"Yes, but I don't want you to let me off that easily," she says, her eyes brimming with more tears.

"It doesn't matter—"

"Shush." Brittany presses a finger against my lips. "It does matter." I shake my head, but it doesn't deter her. "You were right. I was blaming you for someone else's mistakes, and that wasn't fair to you or to Logan—whom I'm very fond of, by the way. I'm sorry I hurt you, and I'm sorry if I broke your trust." I shake my head again, and this time she lowers her hand. "But I promise I'll make it up to you. Just..." Her voice trembles. Grabbing her hand, I lace our fingers together, silently urging her to continue. Her fingers tighten around mine. "Be gentle with me, okay? Because I'm going to fall for you, and I've already had my heart stomped on. I'm not sure how much more abuse it can take."

Bringing my free hand to her face, I cup her jaw. "Well, that's good to hear because I'm already falling for you." Brittany's face lights up, the dimples in her cheeks popping out. Warmth radiates through my chest, slowly seeping outward. "I'm not sure what life has in store for us, but I can promise that you won't regret this. You won't regret us, and you won't regret me."

Closing her eyes, she nuzzles her cheek in the palm of my hand. "Just promise me one thing," she says, her lids fluttering open.

"What's that?"

"If at any point you're not happy or you have feelings for someone else, just tell me. Please don't stay with me out of obligation or fear. Just be honest. That's all I need."

"I can do that," I whisper. "As long as you'll promise to do the same."

She pulls her hand out of mine and then slowly
slides both of them up my chest. "I promise." Gripping
the material of my shirt, she crashes her lips against
mine. My lips part as she devours me, and there really
is nothing else I can do other than go with it because I
need her so much right now.

Planting my hands on her ass, I hoist her up. She
wraps her legs around my waist, the warmth of her
body pressing against my cock. My chest rumbles and
I rip my mouth from hers. "Is this the point where we
get to have crazy hot make-up sex?"

Her swollen lips part. "Yes," she says, breathless.
"Make-up sex. Great idea. What the hell are you waiting for?" Running her fingers along my scruffy jaw,
she pushes her hands into my hair and fists it. Her hot
mouth attacks my neck, and what little control I had
left snaps.

I have no idea what I did to deserve this little spitfire, but no way in hell am I letting her go again.

Epilogue

Brittany

Several months later

"**A**RE YOU SURE ABOUT THIS?" CONNOR ASKS, prepping the underside of my left forearm.

Leaning forward, I kiss the top of his head. "Of course I'm sure about this. I trust you."

His beautiful blue eyes peek up at me. "I know you do, baby. All right, here we go. It shouldn't take long at all."

Sitting back in the chair, I close my eyes. The tattoo gun buzzes to life, and I flinch when it first touches my skin. Connor said this would be a sensitive spot, and it definitely is, but the pain seems to be dulling with each pass.

I knew it was time for my next tattoo. My previous two are linked to not-so-great memories. They're there to remind me about my past and what I've overcome. This time, however, I wanted the tattoo to reflect a really great memory. Last week, Connor told me he loved me for the first time. I felt those three words deep down in my soul, and of course I returned them.

Connor is it for me; I have no doubt about that at all. And what better way to celebrate our love than with a new tattoo. Something to remind me every single day that taking a chance on Connor was the best decision I've ever made.

It must've been something that Connor had been thinking about too, because as soon as I mentioned it, he said he had the perfect idea. I went with it. Connor knows me better than anyone, and my trust in him is unwavering.

So here I am letting the man I love give me a tattoo, and I have absolutely no idea what it's going to look like or what it's going to say. I gave him two stipulations; the tattoo had to be in a different language, just like the other two, and I wanted it on the underside of my forearm, straight down from my pinky.

Time passes quickly, and before I know it, Connor turns off his tattoo gun. "All done," he says, running a cloth over my skin to wipe off the blood. "You ready to see it?"

I nod excitedly, and he turns my arm so I can see the three beautifully scripted words he's permanently etched into my skin. "*Vivere senza rimpianti*," I whisper, trying my best not to botch the pronunciation. "It's stunning," I say, looking at Connor. His smile is beaming, and just like always, it melts my heart. "What's it mean?"

"That's the best part," he says, bringing his lips to mine. He kisses me gently a couple of times before pulling back. "Do you remember when I promised that no matter what happened between us, you would never regret this or me?" I nod, my eyes welling with tears when I remember the heartache I caused that led to that moment. Grateful isn't even a strong enough word to describe how happy I am that he decided to forgive me.

"No crying." Curving his hand around the back of my neck, he tugs me in close. "It says 'live without regret' in Italian. I thought it would be perfect."

My breath hitches in my throat. "It's more than perfect." Mindful of my fresh ink, I wrap my arms carefully around his neck.

Connor nuzzles his face in my hair. "I'm glad you like it."

"Not like. Love," I say, emphasizing the last word. "I *love* it. Almost as much as I love you."

"I love you too, baby. More than you know."

"Why don't you take me home and you can show me just how much."

Connor growls, his eyes eating me up from head to toe. "That's a brilliant idea," he says, pulling back so he can perform his aftercare on my tattoo. "You're so damn smart. Just one of the millions of things about you that turn me the fuck on."

"Connor. Hurry," I say, wiggling in my seat. My need for this man hasn't waned…not one bit. In fact, it's grown to epic proportions.

"And Brittany," he says, wiping salve on my arm, "just to give you some warning so you can prepare yourself…" I look at him questioningly, wondering what he's going to say next. "I'm going to ask you to marry me and it's going to be soon."

My heart stutters to a stop, flops around inside my chest, and then restarts, kicking into high gear. "Not if I ask you first."

Connor's head snaps up, a shit-eating grin plastered to his face. "Well played, babe," he says. "Well played."

Pursing my lips, I give him a smug little smile.
I think I'm going to like playing this game.

THE END
(Or is it?)

Acknowledgements

First and foremost, I have to thank my husband, Tom. The endless amount of support and encouragement you give me while writing is truly amazing. Thank you for making sure the house stayed clean, the laundry got done, and the kids were fed. Thank you for taking over nighttime duty so that I could stay up late and write. Your love and support is what gets me through the day and I'm so incredibly thankful for you.

To my dear friend, Liz Berry. One of the highlights of my trip to Hawaii was getting to know you. You are such an amazing person and I am beyond thankful for your friendship. Thank you for your advice and encouragement, and thank you for taking a chance and reading my books. I am honored to have Live Without Regret featured in 1001 Dark Nights. Thank you so much for this opportunity.

A big huge thank you to Perfect Pear Creative Covers for creating yet another beautiful cover. You know my vision better than I do.

Stacey Ryan Blake, aka the best damn formatter

in the world, thank you for making the inside of my books look beautiful. And, thank you for putting up with all of my last minutes changes. You're amazing and you're never getting rid of me ;)

Last and certainly not least, thank you to every single one of my readers. Thank you for begging for Brittany's story. I hope you swooned over Connor just as much as I did. Your support means so much to me and without you and I wouldn't be doing what I love.

About the Author

K.L. Grayson resides in a small town outside of St. Louis, MO. She is entertained daily by her extraordinary husband, who will forever inspire every good quality she writes in a man. Her entire life rests in the palms of six dirty little hands, and when the day is over and those pint-sized cherubs have been washed and tucked into bed, you can find her typing away furiously on her computer. She has a love for alpha-males, brownies, reading, tattoos, sunglasses, and happy endings…and not particularly in that order.

If you enjoyed reading *Live Without Regret* as much as I enjoyed writing it, I hope you'll consider leaving a review.

Follow KL Grayson here
Facebook: https://www.facebook.com/pages/KL-Grayson/1403900879892076?ref=hl
Twitter: https://twitter.com/authorklgrayson
Goodreads: https://www.goodreads.com/author/show/8299638.K_L_Grayson
Instagram: https://instagram.com/booksbyklgrayson/
Spotify: https://play.spotify.com/user/12153476535

You can also find her at:
www.KLGrayson.com
KL Grayson Newsletter Sign up: http://eepurl.com/6f12n

Books

A Touch of Fate Series
Where We Belong
Pretty Pink Ribbons
On Solid Ground – a Harley and Tyson Novella

Other Titles
A Lover's Lament

Continue reading for a preview of KL Grayson's third full length novel in the A Touch of Fate Series,
Just For Tonight.

Just For Tonight
by K.L. Grayson

Coming 2016

WE ALL HAVE OUR WEAKNESSES...RICH, decadent chocolate, fancy designer handbags, overpriced stilettos in every color under the sun. My weakness is Benny Catalano. To call Benny tall, dark, and handsome would be a massive understatement. His giant, tattooed, drool-worthy frame sits at an impressive six foot three. Thick dark hair sticks up in every direction, giving him that notorious I-just-had-crazy-monkey-sex look that most women love. And the five o'clock shadow on his perfectly square jaw could bring any woman to her knees. Benny wasn't just smacked with the handsome stick. Nope, he was smacked and then beaten with the Adonis bad boy belt.

My only problem ... *he's playing hard to get.*

I've never had to work too hard for anything, especially not a man. My father is the most influential music producer in the world—I'm used to getting what I want. But if I've learned anything from dear ol' dad, it's that money can't buy happiness and the best things in life don't come easy. And Benny *is* worth having, although the way he's been dangling the goods and giving nothing away, he sure as hell is making things difficult.

The question is, *why?*

What he doesn't know is that this privileged socialite isn't afraid to get her hands dirty. If the man of my dreams is the end result, I'm ready to put in the work to make him mine.

My name is Mia Brannigan, and this is my story.